THE LAND GRABBERS

Doctor Jefferson Potter is sickened by the continuing savagery during the last days of the Civil War. His spirit and his body are worn down by the horror and he yearns for a new life away in the wilderness where he can build himself a cabin. He does indeed find his Paradise after the war is over — but now he must face land-grabbers from Washington. Once again he is plunged into a world of terror and death, and the odds are that this time he will not survive.

CURT LONGBOW

THE LAND GRABBERS

Complete and Unabridged

LINFORD
Leicester

First published in Great Britain in 1997 by
Robert Hale Limited
London

First Linford Edition
published 1998
by arrangement with
Robert Hale Limited
London

British Library CIP Data

Longbow, Curt
    The land grabbers.—Large print ed.—
Linford western library
    1. Western stories
    2. Large type books
    I. Title
823.9'14 [F]

ISBN 0–7089–5380–8

Published by
F. A. Thorpe (Publishing) Ltd.
Anstey, Leicestershire

Set by Words & Graphics Ltd.
Anstey, Leicestershire
Printed and bound in Great Britain by
T. J. International Ltd., Padstow, Cornwall

This book is printed on acid-free paper

Prologue

Dr Jefferson Potter paused in his work, straightening his aching back and mopping his brow with a bloodied handkerchief. God! Would the war never end? It was the same stinking routine, day after day, the never-ending stream of groaning patients torn to pieces and in their eyes, mute appeals for help.

The help was running out fast.

Bandages and cottonwool were in short supply and only used for the wounds of those expected to live. The other poor devils were tended as best as humanly possible, but the dwindling medicines and drugs were now being refused to the terminal cases.

He had still not become immune to the screams and curses of men in pain. Some were like animals. Others just turned their minds inwards and waited

1

for the inevitable. His heart was heavy and sickened, for the brutality of it all was now eating away inside him.

When he was forced to take a respite and feed his body and think of his future, he yearned not for a successful practice back east, but for a log cabin situated on the shore of some lake where he could fish all day and listen to the silence in the great wild outback. He would be done with civilization. Done with women who let men down when they didn't stay home to look after them. He could hardly remember Lucy's face, for three years was a long time . . .

He would throw away the coffee dregs and the dream of a idyllic future with it, and go back to the drudge of a field hospital.

It was 1 April, 1865 and it was going to be known as the Battle of Five Forks in Virginia and by the way the fighting was going, it was going to be a Union victory. But at what cost!

Somehow it didn't matter any more

that some of the patients wore the faded grey and yellow of the Rebs. They were all the same under the uniform . . .

Jefferson Potter looked round for his orderly, while plunging his hands into a barrel of disinfected water. It was pink and he knew that the water was too tainted to use, but, what the hell . . .

'Joe, where the hell are you? I want the saw. This feller's leg is gangrenous.'

Joe looked at him stolidly.

'There's no more laudanum and precious few bandages.'

'Go and scrounge some whiskey then!'

'Dr Meikle is using it to swill wounds.'

'Oh, hell! Then for Chris's sake, knock this poor devil out. That leg will have to come off! Then go and find some of that lichen the Indians use to staunch the blood, and Joe . . . '

'Yes, boss?'

'Send young Ted here. Let him have a bellyful of what's going on. He can stand in for you and he can make his lists of stores we haven't a hope in hell of getting, later.'

'Yes sir!' Joe's enthusiasm for Ted's coming stint alongside a surgeon who was more like a butcher, made Potter smile briefly.

Then he was engrossed in exposing the limb that had to be amputated. It was a Rebel soldier who looked up at him.

'It's got to come off, hasn't it?'

Potter nodded.

'Right. The sooner you do it the better.' The man turned his head away.

Joe hit him, just hard enough to knock him out.

'You're getting good at that,' remarked the doctor.

'Yes, well, practice does make perfect.' Then he grinned. 'I'll away to get Ted.'

Dr Jefferson Potter began his preparations. It was going to be interesting to see how strong Ted's stomach was. There was no time now to think of cool lakes reflecting the blue of the sky, or fish tugging on lines, or that herd of horses he would like to own some fine day when the war was over.

Now it was all sweat and putrefaction and coping with men dying when there was no need for it; working night and day, and not knowing the pure relaxation of sleep; living in a perpetual nightmare, so that at times he was working like a zombie.

Ted appeared by his side, a frightened gawky youth, with a bandage on his head, an untrained soldier press-ganged into the hospital corps because he could still walk on two legs.

'Get a hold of his shoulders and if he thrashes about, cold-cock him with that mallet over there, but don't kill him. This leg might, but we don't want to be responsible.'

Ted gulped, already looking green.

'But, sir . . . '

'Just do as I say, boy. Now let's get on with it!'

1

Jeff Potter stood gazing over the stretch of water the Indians had named Lake of the Smiling Waters. Even after two years living close to it, it never failed to move him. He breathed deeply and felt the familiar calm envelop him. It was his saviour, his life.

He was naked, preparing to dive into the clear water, a ritual he did every day, not so much to clean himself but to renew his energies and give thanks to any water spirit that might be out there.

He was tall and broad, made so by constant exercise, his body well muscled and lithe. He was a different person than the man who'd found this place and recognized it as the true home he'd been looking for.

He dived in, relishing the shock of cool crystal water, making his blood pound around his body. Splashing and diving and making the resident birds squawk and take flight, he was filled with a contentment of which he'd always dreamed.

A water rat plopped into the water. It looked enquiringly at the intruder then went about its business. Jeff laughed and splashed it on its way. That was what he liked about this wilderness, animals regarded him as another fellow being. They were unafraid of man and he was unafraid of them.

He got out of the water and shook himself like a dog and the droplets glinted in the morning sun, then he reached for his buckskins and prepared for a new day.

As he ate his frugal breakfast, he reviewed his life so far. The log cabin he now lived in was built by his own hands. It was rudely furnished with a cot, table and stool and a couple of shelves for his books and a wooden chest to hold his extra clothes. On the chimney breast which he'd built from stones and clay hung two guns. His army Spencer repeating rifle and a buffalo gun. His army revolver hung at his waist at all times, a habit he'd never been able to lose since his days as an army doctor, which he always thought ridiculous as he rarely saw a stranger. The small village of Pawnee Indians and the old Indian shaman who lived at the other side of the lake could hardly be called strangers, and they were people he trusted. So why carry the gun?

He ate his bacon and panbread and finished his coffee and thought of his life before he found this place.

He'd been a nerve-shattered shadow of himself when the Civil War was over, and it had been his friend Joe, his trusted orderly, who had saved him in the first six months after the war. He'd drunk himself into a stupor to forget the horrors he'd lived through. The nightmares and the screaming must have been hell for poor Joe, but he'd stuck by him, bullying him to eat, bullying him to wash and mopping him up when he'd lain in his own vomit.

Then had come the day when he had got drunk in the saloon, the name of which he could never remember, for those times were now just a blur to him. But he'd insulted a gambler and accused him of cheating. Joe had tried to hold him back, had wanted to drag him out of the saloon, but he'd chopped Joe on the jaw and sent him sprawling. He'd stood, swaying and cursing the man who pulled out a small derringer from inside his jacket and, as he'd taken aim, Joe had flung himself in between them.

Jeff's reflex had been to catch Joe and lay him gently on the ground. He'd been cold sober in an instant.

Whirling round, he saw the gambler standing, stunned at what had happened. A roundhouse to the jaw had flattened him. Jeff had knelt sobbing by the side of Joe whose wide-open eyes had a look of surprise, while the barkeep and his swamper took care of the gambler.

He hadn't drunk a drop of hard liquor from that day on. He'd taken a hard look at himself and reckoned he was two stones underweight. His hair and beard were now flecked with grey. His eyes were black-circled in a thin bony face. If he'd been a patient of his in the old days, at a shrewd guess, he would have diagnosed consumption.

But, of course, he didn't have to guess; it was what was the matter in his head. Shell-shock and stress and working like a butcher on poor human beings, trying in vain to combat dirt and disease, lying to young lads that they would live when they didn't have a cat in hell's chance . . . that was what all his nightmares were about.

So had started the quest for his idyllic place, his private paradise, where he could build his own home, fish all day and commune with nature and maybe find a quiet contentment.

Sometimes he was riddled with guilt that he kept his black bag of surgical tools and his chest of meagre supplies of drugs that he'd salvaged, unopened. He wanted to forget he'd ever been a doctor and a surgeon.

In those years when he'd wandered far, he'd become a cowhand, a mule-skinner, a lumberjack and a gambler amongst other things. He'd also done a stint on a railroad, but couldn't stand being amongst so many men.

His nerves screamed for isolation. He wanted the solace of trees and mountains, green grass and waterfalls and an ever-flowing river . . .

He found it at the lake the Pawnees named the Lake of Smiling Waters, deep in the heart of Kansas. It was there waiting for him, welcoming him, holding him in thrall.

He saw the place and cried. It was as if it was reaching out to him, to cleanse his soul of the guilt of Joe's death and to rid him of the war years. He was home at last.

He was chopping logs for his home when he first became aware of the old man sitting on a knoll of ground watching him. The old wrinkled face was walnut brown and his long grey hair was in two thin plaits. A leather thong was knotted above his forehead and an eagle's feather dipped at one side at the back of his head.

Jeff paused, straightening his back and wiping sweat from his brow. He knew better than to speak first. If the old man wanted to communicate he would do so in his own good time. Jeff knew he would be assessing what he saw.

Jeff split logs and made several piles, ready for taking to his proposed site. He'd already marked out the ground and dug up clay from the lake's edge. He was preparing to carry his first load when the old man spoke.

'It would be a wise man who would make his home above the level of the lake. When the water spirit is angry, he becomes greedy and engulfs the land he can reach all around his home.'

Jeff looked straight at him for the first time.

'You mean the place I've chosen, floods?'

The old man inclined his head, a sly smile on his lips.

'That is so. I have known this lake all my life, in good times and bad. Now the lake smiles, but sometimes it can frown and become very angry indeed, especially when the water spirit fights with the north wind. Then, he rages.'

'So where should I build?'

The old man didn't pause to reflect. At once his arm rose and a gnarled finger pointed to a rise in the ground, which terminated in a rocky cliff.

'Build there, where the water will not reach, and the cliff will shelter you from the cold north wind. It will keep you cool in summer and warm in winter.'

'Thank you. I shall take your advice.'

The old man nodded his head and when Jeff looked his way again, he had gone.

He built his log cabin and found it snug as the old man had predicted. They became friends, and old Running Bear would come without warning and sit with him and smoke a pipe and watch the great red ball of the sun go down in the West behind the surrounding hills.

It was a time of peace and healing for Jeff Potter.

But now he was worried. Running Bear had not been to see him for two weeks, which was strange. Sometimes he would bring a haunch of venison or a turkey with him and they would cook it outside on a spit and share it. The old man would talk of battles gone by with other Indian enemies when the Pawnees were strong and numerous.

Jeff never talked about himself. The old man sensed there was something in the white man's past he must forget, but he'd seen the army revolver and the repeating rifle and guessed he must have been in the white man's war. It could wait. Someday, this man would want to talk and unburden himself.

But now there was no old man, no one to talk to, no comforting presence. He'd grown fond of the old man. There was no aggression in him, only an abiding wisdom that came from living so close to nature. He must go and find him.

He had never been invited to Running Bear's lodge, and indeed, out of respect, had kept away from the vicinity during his own hunting trips. Now he proceeded slowly and carefully, his rifle slung over his shoulder, his revolver primed and ready.

He left the floor of the valley and climbed upwards, looking back often at the view of hills and trees and undulating land which could support a mighty herd of cattle or horses. Prominently set, was the stretch of water that reflected the blue of the sky.

He must build a canoe, he mused, as he looked back. Perhaps the old man would help him if all was well.

He came to the ridge of pine-trees and entered the green cathedral-like canopy and listened to the scufflings of disturbed animals as he trod lightly.

He sniffed the air, but could not smell smoke. Again apprehension hit him. The old man was old. He estimated that he wouldn't see eighty again. Perhaps he'd had a seizure.

He came to the clearing where the tipi stood. It was built on larch poles; the covering, ancient weathered buffalo skin still showed faint markings and symbols daubed on with natural dyes in red and green and white.

The tipi was surrounded at a distance by the remnants of long dead fires, at least most of them were, but there were signs that at least two had been been made fairly recently. He kicked the ash as he strode by. There was even the smell of burnt wood still there.

His eyes raked the tipi. There was no sign of life. The fire that should have burned outside the tent was dead too. Most unusual.

17

He stooped and opened the flap and peered inside, but could see nothing in the gloom.

'Running Bear, are you there? It's me, Jeff White Hunter.'

There was movement inside and a groan and Jeff pulled back the flap and secured it so that he could see better and saw the old man lying on a bed of bracken covered by a blanket. He sprang forward, nearly tripping over a pile of fishing gear to get to the bed. Kneeling down, he felt the hot forehead and saw the bright glazed look in the old man's eyes.

'What's happened, Running Bear? You've got a raging fever.'

'Water . . . need water!' the old man croaked, his chest rising and falling convulsively.

Jeff looked around him and found a half-full demijon and ladled out an earthenware cupful. Running Bear drank greedily.

Then, as the old Indian moved his blankets, Jeff was conscious of a smell he would never forget. It was the smell of putrefaction.

He pulled back the blanket and saw the bloodied wound in the old man's thigh. He recognized it for what it was. There was a lead bullet embedded somewhere in that leg and it was slowly poisoning him.

'How did this happen?' His tone was curt, anger against a person or persons uppermost in his mind. Running Bear glanced at him. He didn't recognize the man before him. This was the man he used to be . . .

'There were four strangers . . . white men, riding the range as if it belonged to them. They came upon me suddenly. I was skinning a young stag and they wanted to take it from me. I asked them who they were and they laughed and I picked up my gun but before I could fire, one of them shot me. They took my meat. I hope it gives them fire in their bellies,' he finished viciously.

'Well, now, that bullet will have to come out.'

Running Bear looked at him calmly. 'I would have taken it out myself but I couldn't get at it. You can do it, yes?'

Jeff nodded and the old man watched while Jeff gathered dried grass and small sticks in the hole surrounded by cooking stones and fanned a flame so that larger pieces of wood would burn. Then he filled an old iron pot with water and hooked it on a tripod and waited for it to boil.

'You have done this many times?' the old Indian asked. Jeff gritted his teeth, remembering the butchery and the agony of patients and the lack of hygiene and pain-relieving drugs.

'Yes. I was in the Union Army but I don't talk about it.'

'It is something which festers in your mind and poisons your brain.' It wasn't a question, it was a statement of fact.

'Yes, you might say that.'

'Warfare, whether carried on by white men or red, is nothing but an outlet for brutality. It shames the spirit and

20

turns men into less than the beasts. As a young man, I thought engaging in battle was something to be proud of. Now I know differently.'

Jeff was busying himself sterilizing his knife for the operation. He looked curiously at the old man lying so quietly as if part of himself was elsewhere. The young soldiers he'd attended had groaned and thrashed about until they were a danger to themselves and the men attending them.

'Do you need a drink? Or should I give you a sharp tap to knock you out?' he asked quietly. Running Bear smiled at him.

'Neither. The Great Spirit is within me. He will protect me from all pain. Just get the bullet out, and make me a posset from the herbs you will find wrapped in bark in the small basket over there.' He indicated a round basket that Jeff recognized as one such as women wore when they went hunting herbs in the forest.

He nodded, and proceeded to pour

the boiling water in a bowl and then cleaned the wound and, but for an instant quiver of the muscles in the thigh, Running Bear lay still and remote.

Dipping the knife into more water, he made ready to plunge it into the wound and probe for the lead bullet. It had entered deep and Jeff was sweating before he extracted it. He held it up.

'There you are, a .44 calibre bullet from an army revolver and you're lucky; it didn't shatter your thighbone.'

Running Bear watched as Jeff cleaned the wound and bandaged it with cabbage leaves using lichen to stem blood flow, and binding it with reindeer thongs.

'You have gentle hands, Jeff White Hunter. Now if you will make the infusion . . . ' It was only then Running Bear's voice turned to a croak, and his face paled.

Jeff wondered what the herb was that he was brewing. It had a mighty fine effect on Running Bear after he drank it. Now Jeff suspected that the old man, too, had been keeping secrets from him. It would explain the ashes of bonfires around the tipi, for he knew that squaws who were about to give birth, went into the forest with their women attendants and built a new temporary tipi so that the child would have a demon-free start in life. Then, when it was over, and the mother cleansed and the bleeding was finished, the tipi would be burnt taking with it and purifying all negative entities in the small tent.

It also told him why the women came to Running Bear, for he was a medicine man and not just a hermit living in seclusion. He was a holy man and one who would send up prayers for a good future for the new babe.

When he was finished, he sat down beside the old man.

'More comfortable now?' The old man nodded. 'When you are better, we must have a talk.'

Running Bear's eyes studied the

white man's face.

'Why? We both know the important, fundamental things about each other.'

'You're a medicine man and I was a doctor . . .'

'You still are!'

'No! I gave it up when I came out here into the wilds. I'm a man who only wants to forget!'

'You can never give it up. Look how you came seeking me and when you found me, you didn't hesitate. I was resigned to dying when you came. I was ready to go. I owe you my life, therefore, now you are responsible for me.'

'You don't know the man I am, Running Bear! I could leave tomorrow . . .'

Running Bear laughed. 'You could no more leave the Lake of Smiling Waters, than you could pluck your own heart out of your breast! No! Your destiny is here in this place. You mark my words.'

2

Jasper Wirrel drew rein and the men following him drew up likewise. The view in front of them was superb, a long rolling valley, wooded at either side by tall pines and a narrow snaking stream showing silver like a snail's trail.

He turned and grinned at the others.

'See, I told you so! Trust me and we'll all be rich someday. I can see it now, this valley overrun with cows . . . our cows. This land is just there for the taking.'

'You think we'll get the grants, Jasper?'

'Of course. You heard the new governor himself. Clear the land of Indians, and you get first chance of it.'

'But these Pawnees have proved stubborn. The word reservation is bad medicine to them.'

'Aw, Henry, you got no guts! You don't talk to these people, you show 'em! They only know the power of the top dog. Burn a few villages and they soon up and leave. After all, they're a migrating people. If they don't want to go on to the reservation they can go further into the wilderness. It's all odds to me.'

Henry Lassiter looked at Jasper Wirrel with distaste. He'd only known him since meeting him in the newly built government office where new laws concerning the Indians were being made.

Times were changing fast. Now that the Civil War was over and men in Washington could turn their minds to other matters, it was the right time to step in and do the fieldwork for the men at the top and, by doing so, get first option on the rich lands up for grabs.

Henry Lassiter was land hungry. He'd do anything for land, even to associating with this hulking lump of cow dung. He looked back at the four men easing their backsides on their saddles. None of them were interested in what they saw down below. The valley didn't reach out to them. They were quite happy to wait for what the bosses decided. They were morons with no conscience, but muscled morons toting guns.

Three of the men were Wirrel's. The other, Bill Gaffe, had been with Lassiter right through the war. A good fighting man but simple. He'd saved Lassiter's life at the Battle of Bull Run when Stonewall Jackson had made a stand. He'd promised to look after Bill when the war was over, and that was what he was doing now.

As for Wirrel's three followers, he wouldn't give a nickel for any of them. Damn cut-throats, all of them. The way they got together, their talk, and the way they acted, made him wonder whether they'd all been in a gang . . .

He looked at Wirrel. 'What do we do now?'

'Like I said, persuade the Indians to

move on. So we bring in some heavy artillery.'

Henry was appalled. 'We're not at war now, Wirrel! I didn't go along with Swede shooting that old man.'

'He grabbed for his gun! These old 'uns are tough. Once a dog soldier, always a dog soldier! The only good Indian is a dead Indian. Remember that!'

Henry Lassiter turned his horse around. He nodded to Bill.

'We're going back to camp.'

Jasper Wirrel looked at him with derision. 'Getting cold feet, are we? You knew what it meant when you agreed to the governor's plan. He was giving us freedom to take the land in any way we can.'

'I don't go along with cold-bloodedly killing Indians.'

'Maybe we won't have to. Maybe the bastards will see the light and go easy.'

'You didn't give that old man a choice.'

Wirrel shrugged. 'Charlie's trigger-happy. What's done's, done. Anyway, who'd miss a lone Indian with one foot in the grave? Now come on, we'll ride down there and inspect our new lands. We could be neighbours, Lassiter. Your ranch on one side of the valley, mine on the other. What do you think of that?'

Henry Lassiter didn't answer, but rode away, Bill catching him up. Wirrel frowned, watching them He was going to have to do something about that son of a bitch.

Then, looking once more at the fertile valley, he knew there was no way he would share it with Lassiter or anyone else.

They rode on down a gentle incline until, at the bottom of the valley, they came to signs of human habitation. Wirrel could see where land had been cleared for crop stripping, used once and then allowed to go back to nature again. There were fords across the stream where animals and men came for water. Here and there were signs of long dead fires and bits of debris left when a tipi had been taken down and removed.

Yes, he was satisfied. These people were used to moving on. So it would be easy to find the villages, give them a short sharp lesson and frighten them away and, if they proved stubborn, burn a few hovels and kill any would-be heroes and the rest would flee.

Jasper Wirrel rode at the head of his little band, blissfully thinking of the new empire he was going to build.

The tall pines grew in a graceful curve and suddenly there was a new vista, a lake dappled in sunlight nestled nearly to the treeline, its shoreline picked out in white sands.

'Now there's a sight!' he bellowed and pointed. 'I'll build my house down there where there's plenty of room for the corrals and bunkhouses. A gift of the Gods, eh, fellers?'

Charlie Hinde studied the view.

'I think by the look of things, boss, someone's beat you to it. Look there!' He pointed upwards to a knoll above the waterline. Wirrel spun round, eyes glaring.

'What the hell . . . ! Well, I'll be damned!' He was silent for a moment, and then punched one meaty fist into the palm of his other hand. 'We'll soon settle his hash, whoever he is.'

'He's not an Indian, boss, that's for sure. That's a new log cabin and Indians don't build log cabins.' Charlie spat on the ground.

Wirrel cursed.

'We'll have to go and take a look-see and persuade him to leave.'

'Or else?' Charlie spat again.

'Or there could be a little accident.'

Charlie grinned. 'Now you're talking, boss. I'd rather do than talk.'

'We know what you like doing best, Charlie, but hold on to yourself. Take it easy,' he said as Charlie showed signs of becoming excited. 'Art, you watch that buddy of yours.' Art Silvers nodded and drew a hip flask from his pocket.

'You want a quick nip, Charlie?'

31

Charlie grabbed the flask and drank and then sighed contentedly and began to sing. Alcohol was the only thing that mellowed Charlie and turned his mind from killing, for Charlie still lived in the past, his mind not capable of realizing the war was over. He was still a Rebel soldier, now under the command of Captain Jasper Wirrel.

It was late afternoon and the sun was going down over the hills, streaking the lake from blue to golden red, when they arrived outside the log cabin.

'Ho, there. Anyone home?' Wirrel's stentorian bellow startled some birds that flew out of the shade trees in the yard at the back of the cabin, but there was no sign of an occupant.

Wirrel and his men dismounted and cautiously walked up to the door. It opened easily and they stepped inside. The one room was neat and tidy, fishing gear in one corner, a shotgun on a rack and a space for another. So whoever owned this place was out hunting.

He looked at a line of books on a shelf. So the man was educated. There was no sign of a woman living there, so he was either a bachelor or a squawman. That figured. He made a quick decision.

'Fire it! Let's show whoever he is, we mean business!'

He tore a leaf from a journal and found a pencil beside it on the shelf, and scrawled a message.

THIS IS WHAT WE DO TO INTRUDERS! IF YOU VALUE YOUR LIFE GET OUT NOW!

He fastened the note to a tree near the corral with rope and watched as Charlie went around laughing as he set fire to anything that would burn in the log cabin.

When finally it took hold and the flames licked with fiery tongues at the dry logs and the black smoke billowed high above the trees, they drew back and watched from a distance and then, laughing, they rode away.

* * *

Jeff Potter watched the women approach the tipi. One of them was heavily pregnant and in much discomfort. He stood inside, holding back the flap. He turned to Running Bear.

'You've got company, Running Bear.' The old man stirred fretfully.

'It will be Sun-in-the-Morning. It is her time.'

'You've been treating her?'

'Yes. She has had the baby sickness for many months. I have given her herbs. Maybe now she will be lucky and bring forth a fine baby, but I doubt it.'

'Why?'

'Because she is young and fearful. She has not carried well.'

Jeff watched the women begin opening their bundles and deciding on a site for the temporary tipi. Two of the women were older and experienced in these women's matters. One of them looked like the mother of the pregnant girl.

34

She'd been weeping and one of the older women spoke impatiently.

'Pull yourself together, Humming Bird. Nothing bad will happen. Running Bear will make good medicine for her and the spirits will see that she will have a big strong son. You will see.'

'That is the trouble. He looks as if he will be too big for her to deal with.'

'Then Running Bear will know what to do. Come, we'll go to his tipi and consult with him. He must be sleeping.'

They started back as Jeff stepped into the opening of the tipi. The women stopped and stared. Jeff held up his hand.

'I am Running Bear's friend and he is in trouble. He has been shot . . . ' He stopped abruptly as a great wailing went up from the women. He waved his hands at them. 'No . . . no! He is not dead. I am looking after him, but I'm afraid he will not be able to help you.' Again came the wailing and then one of the older women who looked like their leader, stepped forward.

'But he must help us! We want his prayers. Sun-in-the-Morning is relying on him!'

'I'm sorry. Running Bear is in no condition to help you.' There was a noise behind him and he turned to see Running Bear struggling to sit up.

'Tell her,' he gasped, 'that I'll come and say the prayers for the safe delivery of the new life. Tell her . . . '

'But you can't! You're too weak!'

'Lift me up. You are a strong man. Carry me outside so that I can bless the ground the tipi will stand on. All must be right for Sun-in-the-Morning. It will give her courage for the ordeal ahead.'

So Jeff gently lifted the old man and brought him to the place the women had chosen and he blessed it and he watched as they skilfully set up the tipi. Sun-in-the Morning sat close by and Jeff, couldn't stop himself from timing her contractions. He was uneasily aware that they were coming fast.

'I'll put on water to heat and keep the fire going,' he whispered to the old man who nodded approvingly.

He also found some dried jerky and wild onions and set a pot of stew on to boil. The old man and the women would be in need of a good nourishing broth, before this night was out.

He kept himself busy while he listened to what was going on inside the tipi. He felt guilty. He should have made the women aware that he was a doctor and that if he was needed he would come.

But he did nothing, telling himself that at least two of the women were experienced midwives and that they probably wouldn't accept the help of a white man.

He changed Running Bear's bloodied wrappings, noting that the lichen was leaving the wound clean and that no more telltale purply-redness was spreading. Now there was less chance of blood poisoning. He was pleased with Running Bear's progress. He could even think of going back to his cabin. The women could look after him overnight and he would return in the morning.

But he never got to tell Running Bear of his decision. A sobbing Humming Bird was scrabbling at the tipi flap and calling for Running Bear to do something for her daughter.

'What is it?' Jeff opened the flap and looked down at the woman. Her round flat face looked stricken, her eyes sunken and flooded with tears.

'Sun-in-the-Morning is dying. She's not helping herself. The child is too big . . . '

Jeff pushed her to one side without answering and strode across to the other tent. He stooped and entered without waiting for permission. Inside, the atmosphere was already fetid. A brazier gave off light and smoke.

'Open the flap wide and let in the fresh air,' he rasped as the women stood back and stared at him with astonishment, but one of them did as ordered and they stood away from the makeshift bed while Jeff examined the still figure.

He saw at once there was a good time to go, but the mother-to-be was in shock and not helping herself.

'Are you giving her hot drinks?' One of the older women nodded.

'We're giving her raspberry leaf tea and we're massaging her, so what else can we do?'

'Talk to her, encourage her and keep her awake. I'll be back.'

'Where are you going?'

'To my cabin. I'm a doctor and I want my instruments. She'll need help to birth that child!'

He did not wait for an answer. There was no time. If he didn't do something about it, the baby would die before it could be born.

He smelled smoke long before he came to his cabin. He stared at it in shock and a burning fury rose up in his throat threatening to choke him. Who the hell would do such a thing? Then he remembered the strangers who'd shot Running Bear. The bastards must have found his cabin. Heart in his mouth he raced for the corral and the small privy that was at one corner of it. Had they found his black bag and his chest of medicines that he'd put out there so that he wouldn't have to look at them in the cabin?

They were there, in a makeshift cupboard. Thank God, they'd not noticed or realized what the little shack was, or it could have gone up in smoke like the cabin itself.

He looked at the ruins, still smoking. There was nothing left of his possessions and he noted his shotgun was gone. Then he saw the sheet of smoke-blackened paper and read the message. So the bastards thought he could be frightened off his own property?

He thanked God, he'd had the foresight to lay claim to this piece of land. One of the first things he would have to do would be to stake out his holding. No bastard on earth would frighten him off. They would have to kill him first.

But now, he had to get back to the girl who needed him. He was a doctor first: the rest would come later.

Suddenly the icy coldness that had lain about his heart was gone. This time he wasn't working on men who only had a fifty per cent chance of surviving, he would be fighting to save a new life and that of the mother. That was what true doctoring was all about.

He checked his bag and looked through his chest amongst the meagre supplies he had and chose what he might need. Then with a light-hearted step he went on his way, deliberately ignoring the shell of his home. He would face that later.

3

Jeff stepped out of the tipi, drying his hands on a piece of cotton rag. It was early dawn and the sun was just showing in the east. He felt a satisfaction he'd not known since his early doctoring days. He took deep breaths of the sparkling clear air, and listened to the dawn chorus of the birds. It had been a hard night but so worth it; a fine baby boy, weighing at least nine pounds. The father should be proud. He felt a certain envy.

But he couldn't imagine any white woman facing a life of such solitude for his sake. This was a man's world and women didn't survive very long in it. The solution would be to take a squaw and he was no squawman.

Still, there were compensations and this was one of them. He turned and entered the tipi and now Sun-in-the-Morning was sitting up with that tender smile of a new mother on her face and she was suckling her babe.

'Is she comfortable?' he asked the older woman who was brewing a herbal drink, which she'd explained earlier was to promote a good supply of milk.

'Yes,' and she nodded. 'She has much to thank you for. None of us will forget.'

He indicated the brew. 'I should like to talk to you again about your herbs. May I come to your village and visit?'

The woman giggled. 'You may come at any time and I and all the women shall welcome you with open arms!'

He coughed. He wasn't quite certain what she meant but there was a teasing light in her eyes.

'Thank you,' he managed to mutter, then said quickly, 'I'll look in on Running Bear. Perhaps you could arrange for someone to stay with him and then I can go about my own business.'

'It shall be arranged.' Then she caught him by the arm. 'Running Bear has told us of the white men coming and burning your lodge. We are sorry.'

'Thank you.'

'You will not go away?'

'No. I shall build another cabin before the winter sets in. It is my home and I shall fight to keep it!'

He made a brief visit to Running Bear who wanted the details of the birth, the size of the child and how it should be named.

'Storm at Dawn, as his birth name.' He nodded with some satisfaction. 'He stormed into existence like a hurricane when he decided to come. Yes, I shall recommend Storm at Dawn.'

Jeff left him muttering to himself and made his way back to his burnt-out shell of a cabin, quite unaware of the women watching him walk away.

He surveyed the ruin when he returned, hoping something could be salvaged, but the fire had done a good job. It was as if his whole past had been wiped out. From now, it would be a new beginning.

He made a fire and sat huddled about its warmth and considered his situation. At least he had his rifle and his revolver with some ammunition and his black bag and chest of medicines. There was also the corral and something more vital, he had his army severance pay safe in a bank back in Washington. He wasn't exactly down and out and, of course, he had title to this stretch of land.

It cheered him and he rolled over and slept.

When he awakened, the sun was high. He rubbed his eyes and sat up, bewildered, for it was the strange noise of something being dragged that had startled him awake. Hand on his revolver, he looked about him and saw a row of silent Indians squatting before him, impassively watching a band of youths bringing in several piles of sawn pine logs.

'What the hell . . . ?' Then he

stopped as a tall proud Indian arose to his feet and stalked up to him and stood with legs apart, staring down at him.

'You are the medicine man who saved my woman and our son?'

Jeff blinked and looked up at him.

'I am.'

'Then I thank you and I am under an obligation to you and now we build you a new cabin.' He gestured around him at the Indians who were listening and watching with interest.

'But . . . '

The Indian interrupted him.

'I have spoken. You will direct us and we shall cut and haul the logs and build at your direction. Yes? We build in a day.'

Jeff laughed. 'It took me six weeks.'

'We are many. We build in one day.' And they did. They cleared away the debris and built a huge bonfire and got rid of the charred remains, Jeff pegged out the new cabin and they started and worked as teams. Then they did something strange; his new Indian friend calculated that the new doorway should face the east and the morning sun to bring him luck. Before, his door had faced south-east and by the past events it had not been lucky. Maybe these red men knew something he didn't know!

The Indians lined up just as the sun was going down in the west. They were relaxed with Jeff and he now knew something about them all. His new friend was sub-chief Pana Hokan, son of a Pawnee chief of the village closest to the lake. There were many villages scattered in this land, and Pana Hokan told of much unrest because the white men in Washington were sending out representatives to sweep the land free of Indians. They talked of putting them on to reservations many miles away.

So that was why his cabin was fired! Jeff felt again the burning anger he'd felt when he first saw the carnage. Now, as he faced the lined-up Indians, he felt a sense of brotherhood.

'Thank you all for what you have done today.' Seeing that some of them did not understand, he turned to Pana Hokan. 'Please give them my thanks and tell them that if at any time I can help any of you, I shall.' Pana Hokan bowed and turned to his men, harangued them and they smiled at Jeff and then turned and somehow just disappeared into the undergrowth. Pana Hokan was the last to leave.

'Again I thank you for my woman and son. You are welcome in our village at any time. You are our brother.'

Then Jeff was alone in his new cabin. True, he would have new furniture to make, but for now there was a bed of bracken on spruce branches which proved more comfortable than his old bed. He decided to keep that.

He found a leather bag stuffed with pemmican, that tasty food made up by the squaws to last on long journeys. He was hungry and it tasted good.

Then tired with the day's activities following the hard night's confinement, he rolled into his bed and slept the clock round.

The morning brought fresh surprises. Two Appaloosa horses grazed in the corral. A quick examination proved them a stallion and a mare, and they were quickly making friends with his old army horse. He grinned. That chief sure wanted him to remain on this land and breed horses!

Suddenly he had the warm feeling that the bad years were behind him. That never again would he have those earlier nightmares of hacking off limbs that should never have festered. That he'd done his grieving over Joe and the guilt would grow less as the years passed, and that the new cabin was truly a symbol of a new start. No longer did he wish to hide himself away from people and civilization.

He was ready to fight for his rights and for the rights of others. He was being welcomed into a new world!

But first he had to go and face those bastards who thought they had a right to walk all over him and the Pawnees. He would go to the Indian village and propose taking a delegation with him and letting those white sons of bitches see that they wouldn't be intimidated.

He rode over, trying out the stallion who proved unruly and difficult but a good mover. He would soon have him trained as a good army horse should be.

Pana Hokan was glad to see him. He was easy to locate as his lodge was the largest and most ornately decorated in the village. At once they sat down beside a central fire and without verbal orders, the elders of the village silently took their places as in council. The peace pipe was handed around, and Jeff took a puff and choked a little, but no one appeared to notice. Then Pana Hokan nodded to Jeff and spoke.

'You have come to talk with us. We are here to listen as you have proved to be our friend. Please do so.'

Jeff cleared his throat while he prepared himself to speak. It was crucial that he made himself quite clear. He was not out to instigate a war. He wanted only justice for himself and the Pawnees who'd lived on this land for thousands of years.

'Is it about the white men?' Pana Hokan probed gently.

'It is. I am planning to go and face them in their own camp. They say they are government representatives but I think they lie. I think they are opportunists, or why shoot Running Bear at will or burn down my lodge? Those are not the acts of government men.'

'There are also other acts of aggression. Two of our braves have been beaten and sent with messages to pack up and leave. A small village beyond the hills has been burned to the ground and horses and livestock scattered. The message is clear. They want our land.'

'Have you thought what you must do about it?' Pana Hokan straightened his shoulders and looked grim.

'We are not ready to fight, but if we have to, we shall.'

'It may not be necessary. A delegation to Washington may draw the teeth of these men.'

'But that would take many moons. Much bloodshed could take place before then.'

'I can go to these men and talk. I can even go to Topeka or Wichita and send talk over the telegraph wires to Washington.'

Pana Hokan looked interested and some of the elders listening looked from one to another. Some understood what was being said, others looked blank. Pana Hokan interpreted Jeff's words and the listening men looked impressed.

'But do you have the authority? Will those men listen? I think, Jeff White Hunter, you may get a knife in your back or a bullet between the eyes!'

'Nevertheless, I shall go. Burning my cabin makes it my business.'

'Then I shall come with you and so

will my young men.'

And so it was that Jeff rode by Pana Hokan's side with ten of his young warriors behind him. They came to the camp of the white men and stood in line within shouting distance.

It was a slovenly dirty camp. Wagons were pulled into a ring as if the men expected trouble. Inside were the horses, restless and twitchy. Beside each wagon was a jumble of utensils, empty bottles and discarded refuse. Two campfires, still burning, sent up lazy columns of smoke in the still air.

Two men were bending over one of the campfires, setting up a tripod. They straightened up and stared and then one of them dashed over to one of the wagons, shouting as he went.

'Mr Wirrel, sir, Mr Wirrel . . . we got company!'

The second man stood stock-still, hands where everyone could see them. He was sweating a little.

'It's all right, feller, we come in peace,' Jeff said sardonically. 'We want a word with your boss. What's his name?'

The man swallowed.

'Jasper Wirrel.'

'He running this outfit?'

'Yeah, him and Henry Lassiter. Got land office rights to clear this country for settlers.'

'And does that mean shooting anyone who objects and burning homes?'

'I don't know about that, sir. All I know is . . .'

Suddenly he was interrupted by a loud bellow.

'What the hell is all this?' Jasper Wirrel climbed down from his wagon, buttoning up his shirt as he did so. He stared at Jeff Potter and then at Pana Hokan and the row of waiting Indians.

'An Indian lover, eh? Well, you know what we do with Indian lovers! State your business and get out! I can't see you starting a war with that little lot!' He spoke contemptuously.

Jeff gritted his teeth. 'You or your

men burned down my cabin.'

'Oh, so it was yours! Then you would get my message. You'll get out pronto. All this land is designated for ranch lands. The prairies are for cattle and the buffalo must go. That's what the government says, and what the government will get. Savvy?'

'You're wrong. The land on which that cabin stood is *my* land by deed and by law. It also covers the land these people live on and I give them sanction to keep it. I'm telling you now, mister, any more interference from you and you'll have an Indian war on your hands!'

Jasper Wirrel laughed.

'Yeah? And who do you think you're kidding? We got reinforcements coming in the shape of soldiers from the fort. How do you think you'll stand up to them? Think about it, feller. It will save you aggravation if you just pack up quietly and take your Indians and find yourself some other place. We mean to have this land, even if it means killing everyone on it and razing it to the ground!'

'You're mad!'

'Not mad. Land hungry, and we're doing it legit, which makes us bosses of the pile. Get it?'

Just then Henry Lassiter joined them. He looked worried. He'd heard all that was being said. He didn't like the situation whatsoever.

'Might I say a word, Jasper?'

'Yeah. You have your say, Henry, not that it will mean much!'

Henry gave Jasper a glance of dislike which Jeff noticed. So everything wasn't quite all sunshine and flowers between the men.

'May I ask who you are, mister?'

'Jeff Potter is the name, and this is Pana Hokan, chief of the Pawnees in these parts, and you're Henry Lassiter, I take it?'

Henry looked startled.

'Yes, as a matter of fact I am. I'm also a surveyor and a prospector. I represent a number of speculators . . .'

'Ah, now I'm getting the picture. Government bosses getting in on the land grab. The lands around Abilene and Wichita are already proving rich hunting grounds. Now they've got their sights on what have always been Indian grounds.'

'But if what you say is true, Mr Potter, you too are a land owner.'

'Yeah, but not to the extent your land-grubbing friends are after. I only want to live quietly and allow my neighbours to live in the way they have always lived.'

'Have you never heard of the word, progress, Mr Potter?'

'Enough of this crap,' Jasper Wirrel butted in rudely. 'You've got forty-eight hours to get that village moving and then we come in shooting!'

Suddenly Pana Hokan's rifle fired into the air, and Jeff's horse and that of the Indians, danced and jigged nervously.

'In forty-eight hours, that will be our answer!' boomed Pana Hokan. 'What do you think we are? Some spineless creatures that crawl at your feet? Guard yourself, white man, for surely you will find a Pawnee bullet!'

Then, his horse reared on his haunches and he turned and raced away, the Indians following in a whirlwind of dust. Only Jeff remained.

'Well?' said Jasper Wirrel. 'Does the thought of the soldiers change your mind?'

'Not a bit. I was in the army and a detail of recruits doesn't scare me. They crap like everybody else!'

'So you'll fight then?'

'Yes, if I have to.'

'Good. Then I shall look forward to seeing you in forty-eight hours!'

'I too will look forward to that!'

Jeff seethed with anger as he rode away. The confrontation hadn't done any good but at least he'd seen the opposition. There were at least twenty men in the camp who had showed themselves. All looked like professional gunmen. Wirrel had chosen his men with care. It was going to be a tougher proposition than he'd expected. He doubted very much the story about the soldiers. In any case, it was common knowledge that the forts were defended by raw recruits out to learn the rudiments of battle. The veterans were the elite and stationed at strategic points considered important by Washington.

Pana Hokan rode like the wind, the dust devils swirling behind the band of horsemen. He had the feeling that he had lost face with his own men. If it hadn't been for Jeff White Hunter's caution, he would have attacked the white devils. The fiery members of the tribe would already be thinking that he, Pana Hokan, was becoming soft, afraid of the government men, loose bowelled, yellow-stripped.

He was angry with Jeff White Hunter but more so with himself. His confrontation with the white men should have come at a time of his choosing. Now the big white devil called Wirrel thought he knew what he was up against. But there was still time to give the arrogant crawler-in-filth a nasty shock. Two cycles of the sun, he'd said, then they would come with their fire power. Well, they'd be ready if the spirits of the earth, the forest and the water, willed it. Even the wind would blow in their favour!

By the time they returned to their village, he knew what he had to do and to hell with what Jeff White Hunter wished! There would be no more pow-wow. It would be all-out war!

The drums startled Jeff. They echoed around the hills until they seemed to come from every quarter. He was attending Running Bear and had just changed his dressings and, for once, the old man was sitting with his leg outstretched on a log of wood. He was smoking his pipe. He looked content.

But the sound of the drums made him frown and he put down his pipe and looked at Jeff.

'You didn't say Pana Hokan was summoning a full meeting of the tribe?'

'I didn't know it. He left the camp in a hurry. I never caught up with him. He was angry . . . very angry.'

The old man sighed. 'He is an impulsive young man. He would much rather do than think. This is not the time to encourage an uprising. I think I shall have to be present at the meeting. Will you take me there?'

'Of course, but will Pana Hokan resent me being there?'

'Why should he? You are our blood brother. Your opinions are just as important as any member of the tribe. He will expect to see you.'

'Look, you know my view. This matter should be dealt with between the man Wirrel and ourselves. If we can persuade him to leave this country and go . . . '

The old man shook his head. 'Only resistance will make him go. Talking will not persuade a man of his kind. Talking is weakness.'

61

'Then what do you think we should do?'

'Deal with him ourselves and not bring in the tribes. Humiliate him, let him see that a handful of Indians are enough to send him running!'

'But how do we do that?'

'Send our best trackers into his camp and take him! Shaki, the grandson of my first wife's brother moves like a faint breath of wind. He could bring him out.'

'And then what?' Running Bear smiled.

'There are ways of humiliating him. He will want to die!' And that was all he would say on the subject.

The drums moved to a higher note as the shadows lengthened.

★ ★ ★

Back at the camp, the men grew uneasy and bad tempered as the drums continuous beat hammered into their skulls.

Jasper Wirrel prowled up and down like a caged mountain lion and his men watched him uneasily. Henry Lassiter looked beyond the campfires into the blackness beyond and imagined a hostile under every bush. He wished to God he'd never listened to Wirrel's proposition backed up by those lying bastards in Washington. It wasn't going to be easy to send the natives packing and take over land that was designated for them.

He could hear trouble in those drums. They made him nervous and they sure made the men nervous. My God! If they should start another Indian war! It could be like a fire and rage out of control. Then what would those high-and-mighty pen pushers behind their mahogany desks think and do then? One thing was for sure: it would be the likes of us, he thought bitterly, to carry the can. Why the hell had he listened to them?

Then the recurring dream swam before his eyes. Land! The lure of land and the power it would bring. He swallowed hard. He'd always been envious of those who had more than he or wielded more power. But he would never resort to wholesale murder, he defended himself.

He sought out Wirrel who was staring out into the darkness, his mind pulsing to the beat of the drums. He'd show the ignorant stinking bastards who was boss!

He turned sharply as he sensed someone behind him.

'Lassiter! What the hell . . . ? Don't ever creep up on me like that again! I could have shot you! What d'you want?'

'The drums . . . I don't like it. Wirrel, you said the Pawnees would just up sticks and go. It sounds as if they're summoning reinforcements. What if they strike before the military get here?'

'They won't. They like to pow-wow first and posture and dance and whip themselves into a frenzy. I tell you they'll be like leaves in a wind when they confront the army.'

'You're trusting they'll come?'

Wirrel stared at Lassiter. 'Jesus Christ! They'd better! General Longstaff promised he'd send troops to back us up.'

'General Longstaff might be out of touch. He's been a long time in Washington. He's a doddery old man.'

'You know something I don't know, Lassiter?' Lassiter looked uncomfortable.

'He's got a reputation for broken promises. He's old and he forgets.'

'Why the hell didn't you tell me before?'

'Because you said it would be easy. The Pawnees were split up into small villages. Burn down one, you said, and the rest would flee!'

Wirrel cursed. 'And now it sounds as if those small villages might just be banding together.'

'I think we should forget the whole thing.'

'And have all Washington laughing at us, not to mention the shareholders snapping at our heels! It can't be done. We're in too deep. Don't let it be said that Jasper Wirrel couldn't take what he wanted!'

'But . . . '

'No buts, Henry. You've got a yellow streak running right down your backbone, but I'll look after you . . . at a price!'

Henry Lassiter hid his anger.

'So you'll take a gamble the army will show up?'

'No, to hell with that! We'll ride at daybreak and give no warning. We'll burn the biggest village and we leave no witnesses. Tell the men.'

'You can't do that!' Lassiter was horrified.

'What do you suggest then?'

Lassiter gave Wirrel's grim face one last look and then turned away without answering. Sick at heart and cursing himself for his weakness, he went to tell the men.

4

Shaki watched the two white men talking together. Then when one of them walked away and left the big man to prowl up and down like a grizzly bear, Shaki smiled. The beat of the drums was getting to this man. He it was, he had come for. The white man Jeff White Hunter had described him well. He was indeed a grizzly bear.

But no matter, however big and strong he was, he would never hear Shaki behind him, or feel anything after Shaki had pressed that vital spot at the back of his neck.

Shaki was proud of his ability. It had been a secret passed down from father to son for many generations. Shaki could paralyse any man at any time, providing he could creep up on that man. That was why he could move like a breath of wind and not shake the dew from a water lily . . .

Jasper Wirrel never knew why suddenly his legs collapsed under him or the world suddenly blacked out, but he came to tied to an Indian pony, his head lying along its mane. There was a singing in his ears and the back of his neck hurt.

What in hell? He tried to raise his head but it was too heavy. From the corner of his eye he saw a head crowned with a red headband and eagle's feather. The Indian must be loping beside the pony.

The youth caught his eye and grinned.

'White man not hurt bad. Just uncomfortable. Soon get use of his legs.'

'Who are you?' Wirrel managed to mumble, but he couldn't quite get the words out properly.

The Indian only grinned again and loped on, the pony's reins in his hand.

Wirrel's head was clearing. He'd

have the sentry's guts for this! How in hell had this little runt of an Indian managed to get into camp, knock him out and hoist him on his pony and make off with him, without making an uproar? Someone would pay for this and then a cold hand clamped itself about his heart. Maybe he'd never see the camp again!

His bowels erupted in shock. The Indians had got him and everyone knew what Indians did to white men. Slow fires and staking out for the ants to eat were two things that came to mind. His men wouldn't miss him until dawn when they were ready to move out.

He closed his eyes and tried to pray but couldn't think of the right words. He'd never been a praying man. Then he was being pulled roughly off the pony and collapsed on to the ground surrounded by a motley band of Indians who were now daubed and painted with symbolic signs and figures.

Pana Hokan with old Running Bear limping beside him, came to stand before him. The chief, in a tufted war-bonnet of eagles' feathers looked like a giant to the crouching man on the ground.

'You are the chief of the white men who come and make camp on our land?'

'Yes . . . er . . . no. There is another white man who is in charge,' Wirrel gabbled frantically. 'I only carry out orders. I swear to you on my mother's life . . . '

Running Bear spat contemptuously on the ground a foot from Wirrel's hand and Pana Hokan laughed.

'Now you are not the strong man who blustered and threatened us when we came with Jeff White Hunter to talk to you in peace! You now have the smell of a man who cannot control his fear. What do *you* think we are going to do with you, eh? Treat you like the animal you are?'

'I beg you! Whatever you want, we'll

do, but don't kill me! I've got a wife and a family . . . '

'And so have we. All those you would drive away from our own lands, have wives and families. You burned down our white brother's cabin.'

'That was a mistake! I assure you, if I'd known . . . '

'Ah, you make me sick to my stomach! You grovel like a hissing snake and are just as dangerous! What shall we do with him, brothers?' Pana Hokan's hands went into the air and those around him jeered and laughed and the hooting and catcalls began and one old woman came at him with a wide-bladed knife and slit his trousers and, with a grin, wielded the knife around his groin, and then dashed away laughing as he closed his eyes in anticipated agony.

His heart pounded. They were going to castrate him! That was the message in that dirty stinking squaw's eyes. God in Heaven! They were going to turn him over to the women who gloated in that kind of thing. He'd heard tales from the barracks about what Indian women could do to a man.

He felt a fierce pain in his guts. So it was starting. Then he looked down and found himself crapping uncontrollably.

They dragged him to his feet and tore off his clothes and he stood there, humiliated and exposed in his own filth.

The Indians around him laughed and jeered and pointed, and all the while the drums beat their message in the background.

Then Pana Hokan spoke.

'Jasper Wirrel, you will become the great white man who told himself that he could frighten the Pawnees, but found that he couldn't even control his own entrails! He will become a legend in our tribe so that even our babies will be entertained. You are spared this time because we want peace and we bear no ill-will with your government in Washington. But if you come against us, once more, then we come out fighting and there will be no quarter. You understand?'

Jasper Wirrel nodded, listening to the catcalls all around him and there was hate in his heart. His humiliation was devastating. But there was more to come.

They hoisted him on an old worn-out mule and tied his ankles under the beast's body. His hands were tied behind his back and then they smeared his body with the stinking grey-black mud from the river and sprinkled the newly plucked feathers from a cockerel and fixed the rooster's tail feathers to his crotch.

Then, to give him the final touches they hung a cow's entrails about his neck . . .

★ ★ ★

Henry Lassiter stretched and yawned and suddenly he was wide awake as he heard yelling and shouting beyond the camp. Grabbing his gun he crawled from his blankets and dashed outside in his long johns. And stopped short along with the rest of the camp. They watched with awe and silence as a row of Indian warriors on ponies stood silently as one of their number slapped a bony mule's rump and it trotted into camp bearing a naked man with his head hanging down. A pile of stinking offal swayed and dangled on his mud-plastered body along with a thick sprinkling of feathers.

It was a sight that was talked about for years.

Then the Indians wheeled their horses, gave a triumphant whoop and galloped away.

For a long moment, Henry Lassiter was paralysed with shock and then he wanted to laugh and the agony of controlling it sent him into the trees.

'Lassiter! Where the hell are you going?' boomed Wirrel, and the frightened mule did a half-hearted dance and Wirrel slipped a little and the smell about him erupted into the morning air.

'Gotta crap. I'll be back.'

'Then someone else cut me free!' he howled, but there were no volunteers. Everyone sloped off, remembering things they had to do.

Henry Lassiter came back and coolly looked him over.

'Looks like you've more than just a yellow streak down your back, Wirrel. It looks like shit to me!'

'None of your funny jokes, Lassiter. Just cut me free.'

'How much is it worth, Wirrel?'

Jasper Wirrel spluttered. 'By God! I'll not forget this, Lassiter.'

'Neither will I, Wirrel, neither will I. Make it a thousand bucks and I'll cut your ankles and your wrists free.'

'Blast you, you son of a bitch! I'll pay you.'

'Now, before I cut you free or I'll trounce that mule that hard, it'll not stop before he runs into Wichita!'

Wirrel breathed hard and then said

between his teeth.

'There's a thousand in my bedroll. Get it!'

Lassiter grinned. 'Now you're being sensible,' and went off and found the cash.

5

Jeff Potter was hunkered near his outdoor cooking fire when he watched Running Bear swing himself across the rough ground on the two crutches Jeff had made for him.

He concealed a smile behind a battered tin mug of coffee. He remembered the look of contempt the old man had given him when he'd presented the crutches. He'd barely looked at them but lifted his grey-bristled chin and said proudly, 'I don't need the white man's props! I can manage very well.'

But Jeff had noticed that during the days ahead, when Jeff had visited to see to the wound, that the crutches had been within reach, even though they were never referred to again.

Now Jeff ignored the use of the crutches.

'Want some coffee?' He didn't wait to pour out a mugful.

Running Bear sat down beside him and put his hands to the blaze and then took the offered tin mug. He sipped gratefully.

Jeff waited. It was no use questioning Running Bear. He had his own way of coming to the reason for his visit. This time Jeff could see he was bursting with some news for the old man's usually dour expression sparkled with malicious mischief.

'It is a good day to be alive,' Running Bear offered.

'Yes. Any trouble with your thigh?' Jeff marvelled how soon the bullet wound had healed and would dearly have liked to know the mixture of herbs used by Running Bear, but all he would say was that the concoction was made up of his ancestors' recipes going back thousands of years. There was a strong smell of garlic in it, but the other odours defeated him. Maybe some day Running Bear would give him the secret. Now he waited.

'Want something to eat?' It was said casually as a politeness, rather than a hint that the old man was too old to hunt.

'Thank you, no. The coffee, it is good,' and he held his mug for a refill. Jeff gave himself a refill and they both stared across the lake, silent and companionable. Then Running Bear moved and spoke.

'Last night when the moon was high, there was a sight never to be seen again.'

'Oh? And what was this sight I shall never see?'

Running Bear laughed and proceeded to tell him of Shaki's kidnap of Jasper Wirrel and the humiliation he suffered. But Jeff didn't laugh as Running Bear expected. He looked at Jeff gravely at the finish of the tale.

'You do not see the subtleness of it, my son?'

'Oh, I see that very well indeed. But

a white man like Jasper Wirrel will not let such an insult go by. Mark my words, even now he will be plotting his revenge.'

'You do not think he will ride away, back to his own kind and leave us alone, despite Pana Hokan threatening him with war?'

Jeff Potter sighed, thinking of the might behind the military machine.

'You do not understand, Running Bear. Even if all the villages unite and send out an army of braves under one leader, they will still lose in the end. Then the best of your young men will be gone. A tribe can only flourish if all their men survive.'

'Then you think we should go? Leave our lands and act like cowards? Shame on you, Jeff White Hunter!'

'No, I didn't say that. I was only pointing out that a man like Wirrel will take his revenge.' He looked straight at Running Bear. 'Pana Hokan made a mistake. He should have killed Wirrel.'

'But Pana Hokan didn't want trouble!'

'But that's what he's got, isn't it? If he had been killed, the other white man, Lassiter, would have struck camp and gone. I sensed that those two held different views.'

'But when the white man begged for his life he put the blame on the other man's shoulders!'

'Of course he would! A coward will blame everyone else but himself. No, Running Bear, I fear we haven't heard the last of the consequences of humiliating Jasper Wirrel!'

Running Bear watched as Jeff resumed the task of fashioning a table for the new cabin. He had already made a rude chair and a bench and Sun-in-the-Morning had shyly brought him several brightly coloured blankets and one of them was stretched across one wall which brought a touch of brightness to the one-room cabin.

Suddenly there was a commotion and from the stand of trees far ahead came six Indians on ponies. They looked like a hunting party for one of them had a small buck slung across his pony's neck.

Running Bear reached for his crutches and stood up while Jeff threw down his hammer and waited for the riders to come near. But they were astonished to see two covered wagons come out of the bush and pull up with a squealing of brakes behind the row of Indians.

'What the hell . . . ?' Jeff muttered to himself and then stepping forward, motioned Running Bear to stay where he was.

He put up a hand, palm forward in greeting. He didn't recognize any of the visitors but they were Pawnees by their clothes and markings.

'You are White Hunter, white brother of the Pawnees?'

'I am.' Jeff bowed his head. 'And you are?'

'I am the chief of this hunting party, known as Mighty Elk. We bring you white people who need your help.'

Jeff looked past him to the two wagons. He could see the leading driver, who was bent forward with his head on his chest.

'Why do they need help? Why bring them to me?'

Mighty Elk hesitated and then spoke.

'There are families in the wagons and the children are suffering from the white man's scourge.'

'You mean . . . ?' He started forward and the Indians on their ponies kneed their animals well away from the wagons. Mighty Elk nodded.

'They were driving straight for our village, not aware of us. We know that the scourge can kill us all. We have brought them to you as their medicine man.'

But Jeff wasn't listening. He was holding the first driver in his arms, noting the blood caked on his shoulder and the man's dry lips. Then he was pulling aside the canvas top and gazing inside at a young girl of about twenty, lying on a straw palliasse and holding beside her a boy of about ten and a girl a little younger. They were wrapped in blankets and the sickly stench of disease hit his nostrils as he looked at them.

Then he was down on the ground and looking at Mighty Elk accusingly.

'You attacked these people?'

'No. We found them as they are now. The man who could speak told us that they were driven from their wagon train when it was known that the children were ill. They tried to join another but were shot at and refused help. They are outcasts, White Hunter. Your people do not show mercy to your own kind!'

Jeff didn't answer. He was sick at heart. He knew Mighty Elk spoke the truth.

'You can leave them here, Mighty Elk, and I thank you for bringing them to me.'

Mighty Elk put up a hand and grinned and then with obvious signs of relief, the whole of the hunting party turned and trotted away without a backward glance.

It was then that the driver of the other wagon came to stand before Jeff. He stuck out a hand.

'I'm Mark Pierce and my wife's inside with the little 'uns. They've all got the measles, even the babby. We've been through hell. We could do with a drink!'

Mark helped Jeff to lift the wounded man from the first wagon and lay him on a bed of bracken beside the cookfire. Then Mark's wife Annie and the daughter of the wounded man helped to make the children comfortable. The baby wailed fretfully and Annie was despairing in her feeding of it.

'I've no milk. What am I to do?' Jeff patted her on the shoulder.

'Calm yourself. Drink well, and with good feeding your milk will come back. In the meanwhile boil some water and feed the baby with water and she won't become dehydrated.'

Then he set about looking at the children, noting the signs of scratching and their feverishness, how one of them was having trouble with his eyes. Then, turning to the older man, he set about cleaning the shoulder wound and treating him for shock and over-exposure.

Soon, with the help of the women, there was some kind of order and it brought back to Jeff memories he'd thought to have forgotten.

And as they all worked, Running Bear sat and watched and took note and smiled to himself.

But he didn't smile later that night when he and Jeff sat late around the camp-fire.

'I'm worried about the village, Running Bear. You will not be able to have your visitors for their potions. Are there any babies due?'

Running Bear looked at him sharply. 'Why do you ask?'

'Because measles is catching. For white people it is just a childish complaint. For your people, it can be deadly.'

Running Bear nodded his head

slowly. 'I have heard of the white man's scourge but I never expected it would come crawling into our tipis!'

'It hasn't yet. We must take precautions. Because you are here, I think you should stay here.'

'But all my medicines are in my tipi!'

'Good! Perhaps you have someone you can trust to use them for the good of the village?'

'Yes,' answered Running Bear slowly, 'I have a granddaughter to whom I have told many secrets, perhaps she could help the women of the village.'

'Then we must keep a lookout, and if someone comes looking for you, we must keep them well away as you give your orders. This place is out of bounds until these children are better. You understand all this, Running Bear?'

'I hear and understand. I will explain to my granddaughter, Sage, and what she must do so that the scourge does not creep into any of the tipis.'

'You *do* understand it not only kills children but the adults too?'

'Yes, I understand, but not why it should be so. Why Indian people and not white?'

'Because white people are immune, Indian peoples are not.'

The old man swung himself away on his crutches, shaking his head perplexedly. Then he paused and looked back at Jeff.

'Then I too could die?'

Jeff shrugged his shoulders. 'You're an old man and over the years could be immune to many things. It is as the Great Spirit wishes it to be.'

The old man grinned. 'Then I shall be safe. Many times I have laughed in the face of the Great Spirit and stared at death and yet I am still here! He saves me for something special!'

Two days went by and it was becoming clear that Oliver Drew was sinking fast. The wound in the shoulder had turned bad. It was putrid and even cauterizing had not stopped the poison from spreading.

Jeff stepped into the cabin where Sarah Drew, attending her brother and sister, turned to face him, her beautiful oval face framed in dark hair smoothed into two plaits, pale and wan.

'I think you should come,' he said quietly. 'I'm afraid he's sinking fast. He'd like to talk to you.'

Without a word, she slipped past him and he stayed to have an encouraging word with both children. He saw with satisfaction that the spots were now drying and not as inflamed. Tom's eyes were still yellow-rimmed but Maisie's eyes were clear.

'I think you'll both be able to get up tomorrow. What do you think of that?'

Maisie ignored the question and said urgently, 'What did you mean when you said Father was sinking?'

'I'm sorry. He's dying.'

Maisie gave a scream and Tom sat upright on the bed.

'We should both be with him!'

'And so you shall, but he wanted to speak to Sarah alone.'

'It's not fair! We should be with him!'

'Look, your father's ill and weak. He can't stand too much emotion at one time. I promise you shall see him. Honest!'

Tom started to cry and Maisie started to tremble.

'What will we do now? Where shall we go? We're going to die out here in the wilderness! I wish we'd stayed back East!' Maisie rocked backwards and forwards on the bed beside Tom.

'Now that's enough! I don't want to hear another word! You're going to be all right. You've got Sarah . . .'

'She's only a girl! She can't take Father's place!'

'She's strong, is Sarah. You can rely on her.'

'It's all right for you. You're a man and used to living on your own. We aren't.'

'There's Mr and Mrs Pierce. You can all travel together.'

'Oh, them . . . they're not even friends of ours. Mr Pierce and Father quarrelled about whether we should turn back when we had to leave the wagon train. Father wanted to turn back but Mr Pierce persuaded him to travel on. I wish we had gone back and then he wouldn't have got shot by the next wagon train coming through.'

Just then Sarah came back looking distraught.

'Children, wrap blankets around yourselves and come quickly, Father's . . . ' She stopped and bit her lip and blinked back tears, and then proceeded to bundle Tom into his blanket. She looked down at his drawn, worried face. 'You've got to be strong now, Tom. You're going to be the man of the family now!' Then she looked at Jeff. 'Doctor, what shall we do now?'

'I'm sorry. It was a foregone conclusion. The wound was too infected and blood poisoning had already gone round his system. I did what I could.'

She hung her head. 'I know you did. Thank you.' Then she was ushering both children to the lean-to that had been erected hastily for the wounded man.

Jeff went to stare out at the lake, so blue and tranquil against the backdrop of purple hills and grey-green forest. It was a wonderful wild country, where a soul could grow at peace. He drew long deep breaths of pine-laden air. So why should man create such havoc with his fellow man?

He thought of Sarah's question which he'd avoided. What *should* they do now? Should they travel on with Mark Pierce and his family? But Mark and Annie had kept very much to themselves during this time, and preferred living and sleeping in their wagon. It was as if they did not want the added responsibility of looking after Sarah and two more children.

Then there was the vulnerability of two lone wagons travelling together.

They would be prey to Indians and white marauders. Had Mark Pierce thought of the risks?

He decided to have a talk to Mark and find out his feelings on the subject. His advice would be to wait until a larger wagon train was passing through to Wichita or beyond. By then the children would be over their measles and they would no longer be outcasts.

Mark and Annie, however, attended the funeral of Oliver Drew. It was short and simple and Jeff spoke the words that comforted Sarah and the children. Running Bear and Pana Hokan stood impassively by while the white men filled in the grave under a huge ancient pine. Sarah and Maisie lay posies of wild flowers on the piled up stones and Jeff and the Pierces left them to grieve.

Jeff nodded to the Pierce children now playing around the wagon.

'They seem much better now?'

Annie nodded happily. 'Yes, the spots have gone and they're eating again.' She sighed. 'I think it was God's way of making us all rest. It's been wonderful not to be moving along in that old boneshaker.' Her eyes skimmed the lake with pleasure. 'I love it here. I wish we could stay and . . . '

'Now, Annie,' Mark said warningly, 'we've talked this out. You know what we planned. We're going ahead.'

The light went out of Annie's eyes.

'Yes, Mark. Whatever you say, Mark.' She turned away and picked up the baby who had been sitting on a blanket playing with a carved piece of wood in the shape of a doll.

'Mark, are you sure about this? Why not wait for a caravan? The Pawnees will keep a lookout up to fifty miles radius.'

'Not after the way we were treated by the last wagon-train boss! You would think we were lepers! No, the Pawnees are friendly in these parts, we'll go on alone!'

'What about Sarah and the children?' Mark looked at Jeff with hard eyes.

'What about them? I can't be responsible for them and I can't expect Annie to look after two more children.'

'She wouldn't have to. Sarah would look after them.'

Mark hesitated and cleared his throat.

'Look, I don't expect you to understand, but Sarah's a damned attractive girl. Annie's a little jealous. The fact is, she caught me kissing Sarah, and that was why Drew and I quarrelled. So you see how it is?'

'Oh!' A gust of anger took Jeff by surprise. What the hell was the matter with him? He was going on forty, experienced with women in the past, had watched various situations develop amongst his fellow officers and hadn't turned a hair, and now he was angry because this man had sneaked a kiss from a pretty young girl half his age! He had to ask the question. 'Did she encourage you?' Mark looked ashamed.

'No. It was done on impulse. She slapped my face and screamed and that was what started all the rumpus.'

Jeff was conscious of an easing of his guts. It was the thought of Sarah wanting to be kissed that had so angered him.

He turned from Mark Pierce so that Mark could not see the relief.

'Then I'll have to think of some other way to look after her.'

'You could marry her! A man needs a woman out here in the wilderness, or have you got an eye on one of these squaws?'

'I'm not a squawman.'

'Then the answer's simple, isn't it? Marry her.'

'How in hell can I do that?'

'I've got a prayer book. I'll read the words over you both and that will be that. I'll do it before we leave.'

'Don't you think we should find out what Sarah wants?'

'Hell! Girls of that age don't know what they want. Just up and tell her.

She'll get used to the idea.'

But it wasn't as simple as Mark made out. For one thing it was embarrassing, broaching the subject to Sarah who looked at him with wideopen innocent eyes that gradually darkened with incredulous shock.

'Marry you? But I couldn't! I don't want to marry anyone! I don't know how you could think such a thing. Besides, you're old enough to be my father!'

That hurt. Surely he didn't look that old? Then he did his sums and decided he did.

'Look, let me spell it out for you. The Pierces don't want you travelling with them.'

'That figures.'

'And you can't stay here unmarried. You've got your reputation to think of.'

'Why? Who would know? I doubt the Indians would care!'

'Well,' he stammered, 'I'd know, and you'd be a source of speculation amongst the young men around here. If they figured you were not my woman then you'd be a target . . . '

'You mean . . . ?'

He nodded. 'It wouldn't always be marriage they'd be after. White women out West who are without husbands have reputations even amongst Indians of being loose and liking it!'

'Oh!' She looked thoughtful for a moment. Then, 'Then you're asking me out of duty. You're sorry for me?'

'Oh no, not sorry.'

'What then?'

Hell! How could he tell her that her firm young body aroused passions in him he'd thought he'd forgotten about?

She saw his hesitation and turned away.

'You are sorry for me. I'm afraid I've put you into an embarrassing situation, Dr Potter.'

He caught her arm and twisted her to face him and he smelled her scent and felt her soft warmth, and then he kissed her. He felt her struggles and his mouth pressed deeper on hers until her struggles ceased. Then when he released her mouth he expected her to slap his face.

They stared at each other, both breathing fast.

'It's not an embarrassing situation unless you make it so,' he said evenly. 'I want to marry you, because I want you as my woman.'

Her blush was pretty to see. She outlined his mouth with her finger and then she smiled.

'I think I should like that!'

And so it came about that before Mark and Annie and their family moved on, he brought out the old prayer book and before a congregation of curious Pawnees, they were pronounced man and wife, while Maisie and Tom stood by their sides as bridesmaid and best man.

6

Jasper Wirrel watched the telltale dust cloud just above the horizon, then laughed, a certain relief in the sound. Henry Lassiter gave him a glance. Had his partner been worried by the delay in military reinforcements?

'They're coming then?' he asked. 'The governor's actually holding to his promises?'

'It looks like it,' grated Wirrel. 'That dust cloud tells us that there's movement out there, and who else would be travelling in this territory?' He handed Lassiter his glass. 'Take a look for yourself.'

Lassiter adjusted the eyepiece and found the gap in the hills and finally saw the grey, hazy puff of telltale movement. He frowned. Something wasn't right. That dust haze wasn't very big for a troop of cavalry. It was more like . . . He looked again and he, too, laughed, and handed back the spyglass.

'Take another look, Wirrel. I think you'll find it's a small wagon train coming through.'

Wirrel cursed and looked again. Now, several slow-moving wagons could be seen through the haze as they lurched their way down the trail towards them.

'Goddamnit! That son-of-a-bitch back in Washington has done the dirty! He swore blind they'd not allow any settlers or prospectors on this trail! God damn him! I paid good money . . . ' He stopped at the look Lassiter was giving him. 'All right, I bribed the bastard! It wasn't quite like I told you. But the end result would be the same! If we play our cards right, we'll get all this territory, and then you'll smile on the other side of your face!'

Lassiter turned away and then looked back at Wirrel.

'What you going to do about this lot?' He pointed with his thumb at the far distant wagon train.

'Tell them to light out. We've got the men to back us.'

'And if they don't?'

'We'll treat 'em like the redskins.'

Lassiter sneered. 'Might I remind you that the redskins as you call them, didn't react as if you were God Almighty! That they . . . '

Wirrel cursed.

'Don't say it, Lassiter. Catch me right and I'll plug you! I'm still the boss and what I say, goes!'

Not from where I stand, Lassiter thought furiously, and that goes for more than half the men. Wirrel was an egotistical, crazy guy with his head in the clouds and too superior to mix with his men and listen to their views. To Wirrel, the men were just paid killers, there to obey orders and do the job of clearing out the country of unwanted settlers, red or white, so that the whole would one day be part of the consortium run by Wirrel and himself and the financiers back in

Washington . . . with Wirrel as boss.

Lassiter cursed the day he first met Wirrel and listened to his smooth tongue. He wanted out and there were men in the camp who felt the same way.

It would all depend on how Wirrel handled the newcomers. He felt tension in the air. He turned to Wirrel.

'I warn you, Wirrel, I won't stand for any more violence!'

Wirrel spat on the ground.

'And what would you do about it?'

Lassiter gritted his teeth at the contempt in the voice.

'I might surprise you yet, Wirrel!'

'Oh, go and read your Bible, you slimy, Godfearing toad! You certainly had me fooled. I thought you had real backbone!'

Lassiter made his way to the camp-fire and squatted down and reached for the coffeepot and poured coffee into a tin mug. An ageing, long-legged cowboy sat down beside him, his grizzled bearded features all concern.

'Having trouble with the boss?'

Lassiter looked at Elijah Smith and shrugged.

'There's a wagon train coming through.'

'Me and some of the boys have seen it. I thought no wagon trains were coming through this area.'

'That's the snag. They're not supposed to and there might be trouble.'

Elijah Smith looked at Lassiter in surprise.

'But they're white. I thought it was only Indians we was hassling.'

'Wirrel's crazy and getting crazier. I really think he'd kill everyone on sight, red or white. He's power mad.'

'Hell! What we going to do? Some of the boys are talking of pulling out.'

'Maybe we should wait until the wagon train arrives and see what happens.'

'And then?'

'Act accordingly.'

'I'll pass the word to the boys.'

'How many can you call on?'

'Seven, maybe eight, depending. All good shootists, but there's nine or ten for Wirrel. They're the ones who've worked for him before.'

Lassiter grunted.

'Just keep hands near your guns, and tell the boys to be ready.'

Elijah Smith sloped off to have a word in private with his buddies, while Lassiter sat looking into the fire. Then, restless, he took a turn about and went to look down the trail. The wagon train was snaking its way nearer and Lassiter judged that in three hours, just before dark, it would be with them.

There was no sign of Wirrel, or Sam Greene. The bastard must be off somewhere, making plans with the bald-headed, two-gun fighter who trailed after Wirrel like some prairie dog.

Lassiter was waiting, all senses alert when the wagon train finally came to a stop just outside the camp-fire's glow. There were seven wagons and most of them had women alongside the drivers.

Wirrel moved easily towards them, a smile on his usual grim face.

'Hi! I'm Jasper Wirrel. Where are you people heading?'

A big burly man got down heavily from his wagon. He held out a hand like a shovel.

'I'm Bert Kiernan and this is my wife, Molly. We're aiming to take up some land and raise cows. It looks good in these parts. There's five families with me and we picked up a family on the way.'

Wirrel frowned.

'One family alone?'

'Yeah, had some trouble. Kids ill and their wagonmaster turned 'em off. There's some bastards out there,' he boomed cheerfully, 'but now they're travelling with us. They're OK folks.'

Wirrel forced a smile.

'Where'd you pick 'em up?'

'About half a day's ride. Why? Do you know 'em?'

Wirrel shrugged. 'Just curious. We don't get many folks passing through in these parts. We're surveyors, working for the government. This is all government land,' he lied.

'Like hell it is!' Bert Kiernan's voice boomed and some of the other drivers came in closer to listen, Mark Pierce amongst them. Bert looked around at the newcomers. 'These fellers have land grants too, mister. We're authorized to stake our claims and as we've paid good money, that's what we're gonna do!'

Wirrel was hard put to hide his anger.

'There's some mistake. Some fool at the land office doesn't realize this land's already claimed.'

'By who, mister? By who?'

'By me and my pard over there,' he said indicating Lassiter, 'and another couple of shareholders who represent the State of Kansas, that's who!'

Bert Kiernan took a deep breath and looked about him and saw some of

Wirrel's men draw near and several held rifles loosely in their hands. Then he heard the unmistakable click of a cocked weapon.

'All right . . . all right . . . ' He held his hands shoulder high. 'Maybe we made a mistake. We'll get outa here in the morning. The womenfolk and the kids need their rest.'

There was a definite relaxing of tension and Wirrel smiled.

'Now that's what I call being sensible. When you get your families bedded down, all of you are welcome to have a drink with us, and no hard feelings.' Then he gave a genial wave and walked away, a strutting arrogant figure, seemingly oblivious to Bert Kiernan's mutterings.

Later, he listened as the men grew talkative around the camp-fire as the gut rot whiskey went its rounds. He pricked up his ears as Mark Pierce told of the impromptu wedding he'd performed.

'It might not be legal,' he laughed,

'but it sure made the doc feel better!'

So the man the Pawness called Jeff White Hunter now had a woman! Well, that was good to know. You could make a man do exactly as you wished . . . if you held his woman captive! He had a lot to think about. The Indians would listen to the white man. He could be the means of ridding this land once and for all of the hostile Pawnee Indians.

When the last man had staggered back to his wagon and everyone settled down for what was left of the night, he quietly awakened Lassiter and Sam Greene to come to his tent.

Lassiter groaned and stretched. What the hell was the bastard cooking up now?

He soon found out. He listened with horror while Sam Greene spat and looked thoughtful.

'That's murder! You can't massacre a whole wagon train! Good God, man, they're white folks!'

'That's the only way we'll get 'em

off our backs! Don't you see, once it gets out that they've staked claims and settled, there'll be a whole stream of 'em coming through. No! What we'll do, is you Sam, and some volunteers make up an Indian war band.'

'And how the hell do we do that?'

'You strip down and paint your bodies with that bark dye the Indians use and daub that blue and white gunge they use over your faces.'

'And how do we get the paint?'

'From the Indian village, dummy.'

'But they'll know it's a trick!'

Wirrel raised his eyes heavenward. 'Jesus! Do I have to spell everything out? We burn down the village first, kill every red bastard there, and *then* go after the wagon train. Savvy?'

Sam Greene marvelled.

'That's a hell of a plan, boss, but it will cost you.'

'I know, but my partners will go along with it. When needs must, the devil drives. There's rich pickings in the future. You tell all those interested that we pay good.'

'And you'll blame the Indians for the massacre?'

'Yeah, that's our excuse for burning the village if any hard questions are asked.'

'What about the doc and the old healer? We can't leave them to talk.'

'I've figured what to do about the doc. We can't burn down all the Pawnee villages, so we snatch his new bride, and persuade him to talk to the chiefs. A man'll do 'most anything to get his woman back.'

'But will he get her back?' Sam looked sly. 'She could talk.'

Wirrel laughed, and Lassiter, silent and forgotten, felt sick to his stomach. He would have to find Elijah Smith and talk to him.

The wagon train moved out at dawn. Bert Kiernan waved farewell as did the other men, who'd enjoyed their impromptu drinking session even though they all suffered from hangovers of varying degrees.

Jasper Wirrel grinned as he watched them go.

'Fools! They won't know what hits them,' he muttered and then turned to Lassiter. 'Round the boys up. We're gonna visit that stinking village.'

'But Wirrel . . . '

Wirrel's Colt suddenly appeared, trained on Lassiter's belly.

'Are you with me or against me, Lassiter? Choose, once and for all.' He cocked his weapon. Lassiter gazed down the barrel and it looked wide and deadly. He choked a little.

'Don't be a fool, Wirrel. There's too many witnesses.'

'Then you're against me, eh?'

'You know how I feel. I don't go along with murder.'

The gun came up, and Wirrel took aim, slowly and deliberately, enjoying the panic and horror and fear that swept in quick succession over Lassiter's pallid face. Then the gun exploded and the bullet hummed like an angry bee past Lassiter's left ear. Wirrel laughed.

'You're lucky, Lassiter. I could so easily have killed you but I need your respectability in Washington.' Then without warning, he punched him in the face and Lassiter's legs buckled and he hit the ground. Then, gesturing to Sam who'd watched the exchange impassively, he said, 'Tie him up and leave him in my tent, and we'll ride to the village.'

Sam grinned evilly. 'And afterwards, boss?'

'You and the boys will get ahead of the wagon train and make for the Devil's Gorge Pass. We'll take 'em there.'

'And what will you be doing, boss?'

'I'll be visiting the doctor and persuading him to help us rid the country of the rest of the pesky Indians . . .'

Sam laughed and kicked Lassiter before binding his wrists behind him, and prepared to drag him to the tent.

'If you happen to want to play games

with the woman, boss, I'd like to be there to share in the fun, being deprived, as you might say, on your behalf.'

Wirrel gave him a long considering look.

'It depends on how the doc reacts. If he proves stubborn, then I might just give all the boys some relief! That would make our good doctor take notice!'

Sam laughed. 'What about saving some of the squaws and having us a real party? The boys would go along with it. They'd do anything for a woman!'

Wirrel frowned. 'No squaws! If the womenfolk are missing when the bodies are found, then the cat would be out of the bag. No, I think it would be best to wait. There's plenty of whores willing to part the men from their payoffs.'

Sam looked sulky. 'Maybe some of us don't want to wait, boss.'

'Jesus Christ! Do you keep your brains in your pants? You're on the verge of making more dough than you've ever seen in your life and you're worriting on about wanting a woman! You make me sick!'

Sam gave him a baleful look and took out his anger on Lassiter by kicking him in the ribs before dragging him away.

There was much laughter and joking as Sam chose the men who would make good Indians. Elijah Smith stood back, watching and waiting and wondering where was Lassiter in all this.

He nodded to several of his buddies and they melted into the undergrowth where they watched the departure of the small band headed by Sam Greene and their boss, Wirrel.

'I don't like it,' Elijah growled. 'What in hell is Wirrel up to? He acts more like a four-flusher than a government agent. I don't mind doing a bit of scaring off of the natives, but what I heard, the man's crazy and he's going too far.'

'I heard Tipton say that they were going to burn down that village, but you know how Tipton talks,' said a big burly blond man with a wall-eye and a limp, who answered to the name of Swede.

'What I want to know is where in hell is Lassiter?' Elijah Smith worried. 'He's my man and if we're going to get a square deal, we'll get it from him.'

'Then we go look for him,' said Swede.

They looked for him at the camp-fire but he wasn't cleaning his weapons with the rest of Wirrel's men. He wasn't at the strea.n or with the horses.

'Smells fishy to me,' one of the men muttered. 'Have he and Wirrel had a dust-up, d'you think? Maybe Wirrel's done for him . . . '

'There'll be hell to pay, if he has,' said Elijah tersely. 'Lassiter represented the shareholders. He wasn't only Wirrel's partner, but here to see that everything was done legal-like.'

Swede snorted. 'Who the hell could prove otherwise out here? Accidents

116

are always happening and those pen-pushers back in Washington, don't know their asses from their elbows, when it come down to sheer skulduggery. Come on, let's find Lassiter or his body!'

It was Elijah who found him. He'd passed Wirrel's tent severl times and suddenly been curious as to what Wirrel might have lying about. He'd opened the flap and blinked into the darkness and sniffed. The bastard certainly had a stash of whiskey with him. He could smell it on the air.

It reminded him of his dry throat. He might as well sample what there was. He grinned. Wirrel wouldn't be able to put a finger on him.

He opened the flap wider and stooped and entered, saw a half-empty bottle and pulled the cork and took a good swallow. Then he looked about him. Maybe there was something he might hold over Wirrel if push came to shove.

It was then he was vaguely aware of

movement under a stash of blankets, and heard a moan which was more of a whimper. He flung back the blankets and stared down at Lassiter, bloodied in the head and still unconscious.

'Holy Mother of God! What have they done to you,' he breathed and held him up and poured some of the whiskey into his mouth. Lassiter choked and groaned and attempted to shake his head.

'Take it easy, boss. I'll get you out of here.'

'Where am I?' Lassiter's voice was a croak.

'Stashed out of sight in Wirrel's tent, that's what!'

Lassiter groaned again and tried to sit up, holding his head which was caked with dark crusted blood. He fell back at the pain in his ribs.

'That son of a bitch! He's crazy!'

Elijah offered him the whiskey again and he drank deeply, gasping a little as the liquor hit his stomach. Then awareness came into his eyes.

'How long have I been out? Where's Wirrel now?'

'Not long I should think, boss. Wirrel and Sam Greene's buddies rode out about twenty minutes ago. There was some talk of them burning the village after they disguised themselves as Indians. Why they should do that, I can't figure.'

Lassiter grabbed Elijah's arm.

'Get me up, Elijah. I can tell you why they're disguising themselves as Indians. They're going to massacre that wagon train!'

Elijah stared at him in horror.

'Are you out of your mind? Why, they was drinking with us last night, and Wirrel waved 'em off this morning all cheery like.'

'Well, I'm telling you, that those picked men of Sam Greene's know what they're supposed to do. That's why some of us were left behind. Figure it for yourself.'

Elijah shook his head. 'See here, boss. You got cold-cocked on the head.

119

Now you just take it easy.'

Lassiter thrust Elijah from him in a fury and rolled on to his knees in an effort to stand up. He rolled drunkenly.

'Goddamnit! If you won't believe me, I'll have to find someone who will! Why else would they dress up as Indians on the prod?'

'So the blame for whatever they're gonna be doing is blamed on the Pawnees?'

'Now you're getting there, and for why?'

Elijah shrugged. 'Now you've got me. Why?'

'Because those were settlers with papers to prove their right to claim land. Don't you get it?'

'But Wirrel told us that all this land was already government-claimed land. You said yourself it was.'

'That's what Wirrel told me. I was duped like all of you. I came along in good faith to do a job for those in Washington. Now I've found out that those we represent in Washington are not government agents but gamblers and get-rich-quick racketeers!'

Elijah reached out and hauled Lassiter to his feet.

'God Almighty! What do we do now?'

'You've got to warn the wagon-train, Elijah, and take some men with you. I can't ride.' He doubled up with a groan. 'I think my ribs are busted.'

'You take it easy, boss. I'll send a man to get that doctor and he'll fix you up fine.'

They made their way to the camp-fire where most of the men were lounging and waiting for orders. Elijah explained what was happening and as one man set off to find Dr Potter, the rest were saddling up to ride with Elijah across country to find the wagon train.

Lassiter watched them ride away, bitter and vengeful. He would get Wirrel if it was the last thing he did.

7

Jeff Potter stretched his aching back and paused in chopping wood to watch his young wife laughing and giggling with her sister and brother. They were playing tag and Sarah looked happy, without a care in the world.

Sometimes he wondered about the twenty years' difference in their age, and the lonely wilderness life they were leading. She never complained, never appeared discontented, and yet he wondered whether it was fair on such a young girl to deprive her of other people and experiences. He also worried about Tom and Maisie. Soon they would want to stretch their wings. They would inevitably want to move on and see the rest of the world. Which was only natural, he told himself, they couldn't and shouldn't stay here with him for ever.

But would Sarah want to go with them?

He searched his heart. Could he sacrifice his new way of life for them? Could he leave the peace he'd craved so long and leave his new Pawnee friends, for a new life in a new community?

The answer eluded him, or was he too much of a coward to face the answer?

He gripped the axe and balanced a log on the tree stump and flexed his muscles and came down viciously on the log, the impact jarring his spine and somehow releasing an energy that needed freeing. The log split and fell apart. He reached for another.

Then he forgot about splitting logs and Sarah's state of mind as he stared at the man galloping a steaming, frothing horse who'd pulled up so sharply, the horse had risen on his haunches.

Jeff threw away his axe and caught the quivering mount, automatically running a hand over sweating flanks.

'Easy there, feller. What's your hurry,

that you'd kill the horse?'

The man slid off the horse and leaned heavily against it.

'I've rode as fast as I could. There's hell on at the surveyors' camp. Lassiter's been beat up and I got to get you fast!'

Jeff didn't stop to ask questions but called Sarah.

'Honey, I'm wanted at the camp. I'll be back as soon as possible . . . and honey, don't take risks. Stay close to home and don't let those kids wander. You hear me?'

Sarah nodded and ran with him to the cabin. He needed his medical bag.

'Is it serious, Jeff?'

'Could be. A man's been beaten up.' He looked at her, and then took her in his arms and kissed her briefly. 'Don't worry. You're safe here. All I want is for you to be careful, that's all.'

'I don't like it when you're away. I feel safe with you.'

He stroked her hair and kissed her again.

'You're happy here with me? Would you rather live near other people?'

She shivered. 'No. I like being here, but with you. I wish you hadn't to go away.'

'I'll soon be back, love. Now you be brave. You've got Maisie and Tom to keep you company. Now I must be off. It sounds urgent.'

He rode away with the messenger, but turned as they entered the trees and waved. She was watching him and she waved back. He thought of her as he rode along. Part of his question was being answered, but they must have a talk when he returned.

Standing behind a tree, his fingers nipping his horse's nostrils so that it made no sound, Jasper Wirrel watched Jeff Potter's departure. His lips twisted in a sneer. Soon, he would have the troublesome doctor helping to rid this vast rich land of the Pawnees for ever.

★ ★ ★

Sam Greene reined in his horse as did the men behind him. They looked down on to a flat rolling plain surrounded by woodlands. Two circles, one inside the other, of Indian tipis surrounded an open space, in the centre of which was a huge carved totem pole. The carved faces looked out on all four sides like huge sentinels Sam Greene thought sourly, for the all-seeing eyes on the wooden masks glared hypnotically.

The half-breed, Blue Jay, kneed his mount forward so he could talk to Sam.

'I don't like it. It's too quiet.' He gazed down at the foreshortened figures around the camp-fires. A few small children played around their mothers, but there was no sign of the half-grown children or the young fighting men of the village. 'Perhaps they're on a hunting trip. The youngsters go along to help bring back the meat and to have a chance at their first kill.'

'All the better for us. We do what we have to do and then get out pronto.'

Blue Jay turned to Sam Greene, scowling.

'And it doesn't worry you that we kill women and children?'

'No, why should it? They're only Indians. Think of your bonus, man. Think what you can do with real cash in your pocket. Think of the women you can have, and the respect you get from being a rich landowner back in Washington. Think man, think!'

Blue Jay nodded, but bit his lip. He'd always hated that sneering look from white men because his mother had been of the Sioux nation. After all, the Sioux and the Pawnees had been enemies for much longer than he could remember. Why should he worry himself about killing Pawnee women? Plenty of Sioux women had died at the hands of the Pawnees. It would be good to flaunt his new wealth and status to some individuals in Washington who'd shown their contempt in the past.

'I'm ready when you are and the boys are raring to go.'

'Right! Let's get at it!' Sam Greene raked his horse's ribs with his spurs and the great horse lunged forward, and went at a break-neck gallop down the hill with the men streaming out behind them hollering wildly and guns ablazing.

The men split into two streams encircling the tents from both sides so that none could escape from the circle. Old men and women and children erupted from the tents and many of them fell as they emerged, blinking and bewildered and confused.

There was panic as young women scooped up babies, but there was nowhere to run to or hide. Several old men had ancient shotguns but they were useless against the attack.

As Sam Greene levelled his gun and shot another moving target, he thought it was like shooting down rats trapped in a barn. He laughed as he saw an old man try to drag himself away. He was screaming and blood poured from a wound in his stomach. Serve the dirty old scalplifter right! Indians were animals. They had no rights to decent land, and everyone said the only good one was a dead one.

He swung his gun around and aimed at a woman heavy with child. Two kills with one shot, he grinned to himself. Then his world exploded. He was conscious of blood and pain and a smothering blackness enveloping him. He turned wide, astonished eyes at the man holding a smoking weapon in his direction. Blue Jay. Why? Why? He opened his mouth to ask, but only a rattle of air escaped from his lungs before he collapsed.

The mayhem went on. The blood lust was on the men and soon, when there were no more targets, they fired the tents. Blue Jay, bearing in mind the plan to attack the wagon train, remembered to look out for the war paints. As usual they would be kept in the chief's tipi.

As the other men systematically fired the tents, he looked for and found what he sought. There were several gourds splashed with colour. He grabbed them and fired the tent.

Smoke swirled, choking, blinding as the flames took hold and then came the roar and heat and the white men withdrew to watch the carnage. The totem pole burned fiercely as the many coats of pigment melted and crackled and it was like a writhing spirit of vengeance, the topmost masks twisting amidst the red licking flames.

Blue Jay had a sense of foreboding. It was time to get away. He had a strange feeling running up and down his spine that they were all being watched.

They rode hard until the sun was high in the sky. Then stopping by a stream, they washed away the stench of smoke and of death from them, and began the task of turning themselves into Indians.

The men laughed and joked, to dispel the horror of reality. The killing lust was over. They now faced the fact that the men and boys of the village would live only for revenge.

The men now looked to Blue Jay for instructions. They recognized him as their new leader. All suspected Sam's killing had been deliberate, for who amongst the women and children of that village had had a gun or the presence of mind to fire it?

Their eyes slid away from him as they waited while Jonty Holden asked the crucial question.

'What we do now, Blue Jay?' Blue Jay shrugged and looked around at the bunch which, at a careless glance, might pass as an Indian hunting party.

'Carry on as the boss ordered. We ride on to the Devil's Gorge and wait for the wagon train at the pass.' He avoided Jonty Holden's eyes.

'You're sure about this, Blue Jay? It's one thing clearing out a nest of Indians, they're no dead loss, but a wagon train? It kinda puts us outside the law.'

Blue Jay laughed. 'What's the difference between red men and white?' He swallowed, as if he tasted bitter gall.

'We stepped over the edge when we butchered the first woman,' he finished roughly.

'Then why did you kill Sam Greene?' a voice from the back shouted. There was a general stir amongst the men, all wanted to hear the answer.

'Because he was enjoying what he was doing. There's a difference, you know, having to do a job against your better judgement because it's necessary, and doing it for love. Sam Greene hated Indians and he hated women. Now if you fellers still want to get rich, you'd better put your scruples away and get riding!'

They rode on, but now it was a quiet brooding group with Blue Jay riding point.

The hours passed and they only stopped to rest and water the horses before moving on. They ate as they rode. Then Blue Jay moving ahead, found the trail of the caravan, the wheel marks of heavy wagons and horse droppings hardly cooled down.

He grinned as he joined the others. 'Only a couple of hours in front of us. We can sidetrack them and get into position in the pass and when they're well into the gap, we can attack. There'll be no turning back.'

The horses were tired and so were the men, but they were heartened by the knowledge that it would soon be over. It would be like taking candy from a baby. They all shied away from the actual enormity of what they were about to do. After all, they'd lived through their first blood-letting.

The sun was sinking in the west when finally they reached the place known by the Indians as the Devil's Gorge. It was now licked with orange and red flames of the setting sun. It was a long gash in a wild landscape, brooding in perpetual twilight as the great sheer cliffs rose on each side of a narrow winding gap that had once been a riverbed and, over aeons of years, water had eroded the sandstone until now it was nothing but a rough sanded trail strewn with rocks which made it difficult but not impossible for wagons to pass through.

All was quiet. None of the watching men appreciated the grandeur of the natural vista. All thought of it as a good place for attack.

Blue Jay grinned at the men.

'You see. Nothing to it. We'll get in there and choose our positions. Let 'em get well inside the pass before we strike. Wait for my signal. I'll fire two shots, quick, and then you go for the wagon right below you. Right? No quarter. We don't want to be exchanging shots. We get 'em quick and good, and we rifle the wagons like the Indians would do. We want it to look right for when the army comes along.'

'What about scalping them?'

Blue Jay hesitated, then said, 'We do that too. Think Indian. We want to point the evidence to the Pawnees, and then Washington might send in extra troops to help us drive 'em all out of the territory. Anyway, that's the theory as the boss told Sam Greene.'

'Where's Wirrel now?'

'Out on some business of his own. He'll be catching up with us.'

'Sounds to me, he's letting us do all the dirty business,' grumbled Jonty Holden. 'If it goes wrong, he's in the clear.'

Blue Jay frowned. He'd not got round to thinking those kind of thoughts.

'Nothing's going wrong,' he snapped. 'Now let's get in there while there's enough light to see and we can choose our positions. They're bound to bed down for the night. It'll be like shooting trapped rats.' He thought again of the helpless women and children whose eyes had opened wide in shock and surprise before the life had gone out of them. Yes, like rats in a trap.

They entered the pass, which was hot and fetid with the stench of underbrush and dampness that never saw full daylight. There were vines and weedy bushes that strained upwards for light. It wasn't a place to linger in. There were noises and slitherings of creatures who lived their lives in semi-darkness.

It was an eerie place and Blue Jay remembered the tales told of Sioux victories and defeats at his mother's camp-fire. Somewhere ahead was the sacrificial plateau where the victors of such battles sent their enemies to their deaths. There were as many Pawnee bones as Sioux bones lying deep down the cleft at the bottom of that plateau.

Blue Jay shivered. It was a cursed place and he was glad when Wirrel, accompanied by the doctor's woman, caught up with them and Wirrel again took command.

'What the hell's the matter?' Wirrel barked at Blue Jay. He glanced at all the men who were now moving cautiously and with some reluctance. 'It's only a pass, for God's sake!'

Blue Jay shrugged. 'It feels like it's haunted, boss.'

'What are you, a man or a mouse? You're all acting like a bunch of frightened virgins!'

Jonty Holden spat between his horse's ears.

'It's a damned eerie place, boss. The boys think they'd be better in twos and I agree. I don't aim to hide behind some rock all on my ownsome and the sooner that wagon train comes along the better.'

'You're not having second thoughts? I'd not like that.' His tone was grim.

Blue Jay laughed. 'No, boss. We're just jumpy.'

'Then let's ride and get into position.'

Up in the gorge, Indian eyes watched their progress as the column of men with the woman rode into the gorge, unaware of the waiting ambush and the hate and savagery ahead . . .

8

Jeff Potter knelt down beside Henry Lassiter, noting the bruising as his fingers delicately probed the man's ribs. He also saw something else, the vengeful temper suppressed by tightened lips and curling nostrils. This man was ready to explode.

'Hmm, you're lucky. No broken ribs but plenty bruised. Might I ask who did this?' He busied himself in tearing up a shirt and forming a makeshift bandage to support Lassiter's ribs.

For a moment, Potter thought Lassiter was going to ignore the question and mentally he shrugged. It was no business of his. These men could continue to half-kill each other and be damned!

Then Lassiter groaned as he tried to move to sit up.

'God damn the bastard! It was

138

Wirrel.' He reached out to grasp Jeff Potter's arm. 'You've got to stop him! He's a devil! Even now he's on his way to your cabin. He reckons you'll rid the territory of the Indians for him!'

'Why should I do that?' Potter was astonished and thought the man raving. Lassiter coughed and gasped, his ribs giving him hell as he did so.

'Because he's out to kidnap your wife! He reckons the Indians will do as you say. A cleared territory for your wife's safe return!'

Jeff Potter jumped to his feet, his patient's needs forgotten. He was thinking how terrified Sarah would be, and there were the other kids to consider.

'My God! I'll have to get back!'

'But that's not all,' gasped Lassiter, 'he intends to fire that village and then go on and massacre that wagon train.'

Potter stared down at him.

'Why should he do that?'

'Because they've all got the go-ahead

from Washington to stake claims in the State of Kansas! And Wirrel reckons that every bit of claimable land should go to his consortium. He had me fooled too. I thought . . . '

But Potter didn't stop to hear what Lassiter thought. Sarah! His mind was filled with Sarah, his beautiful young wife who'd filled a gap and made him whole again. He couldn't foresee life without her. If that devil had taken her and harmed her . . . A searing hot/cold anger swooshed through him, causing him to see red. I'll kill him inch by inch, he thought furiously. He'll beg me to die, and no Indian could devise such a torture as he as a doctor could come up with . . .

He rode like the wind, putting his horse to obstacles rather than going around. Branches tore at him and whipped him in the face, but he felt nothing. His mind was galloping ahead, fearful, agonizing, and as he rode into the clearing before the cabin, he knew coldly that he was too late. Sarah always came out of the cabin to meet him.

There was no smoke rising lazily from the stone chimney.

He flung himself off the horse and strode inside. All was quiet. There was no sign of Tom and Maisie. Surely he wasn't mad enough to kill them? But they were witnesses, and could testify if things went wrong. He knew then, in a mighty flash of understanding, that no matter how much he helped Jasper Wirrel to persuade the Pawnees to leave their homelands, Sarah would never be freed and he would never be allowed to live to testify back in Washington.

He looked around the cabin and then stood at the door.

'Sarah!' he called, anguish cracking his voice. 'Tom, Maisie, where are you?'

He crossed with long strides to the new outhouse he'd built since his marriage for Sarah to wash the linen. Under it he'd dug out a cellar as a cold store. Now he opened the cellar trapdoor and prepared to descend the crude ladder, for he must take provisions with him on his journey to find his wife.

He paused as he heard whimpering. Then his heart leapt and he almost fell down the rest of the ladder.

'Tom? Maisie? It's Jeff. You can come out now.' Into the beam of light radiating from above he watched the two children with arms about each other, come blinking into the light.

Maisie sobbed and tearing free from Tom, held out her arms and Jeff enfolded her and somehow Tom too was being held tightly.

The small bodies trembled with fright and cold.

'There . . . there . . . you're safe now,' he soothed, and soon he had them both back into the cabin and he was coaxing the dying embers in the fireplace back to life and the coffeepot was put on to boil.

When they'd eaten and drunk, he said

quietly and calmly, 'What happened to Sarah?'

Maisie started to cry but Tom blinked hard and knuckled his eyes.

'A man came . . . a white man. I saw him come out of the bushes. You hadn't been gone long and I told Sarah, and we watched him out of the window. Sarah was frightened and said that we should go and hide in the cellar. We climbed out of the back window and ran and he didn't see us. Sarah was getting down the old gun. We heard shots when we were climbing down the ladder. Then I pulled down the trap and we didn't hear anything until you came.'

'So you didn't see what happened?'

Tom shook his head.

'No. Like I said . . . '

'All right. I think he took her away. There's no sign of blood. She must have fired to scare him off but he wasn't scared. Never mind, Tom, you did right to hide. You were looking after Maisie. God knows what might have happened to you, otherwise.'

'What will you do now, Jeff?'

'Go look for her and when I catch up with that snake, I'll . . . ' He gulped and remembered he was talking to children. 'I'll make him pay,' he finished lamely.

'What'll happen to us?' Tom looked about him uneasily.

'I'm taking you to Running Bear. You'll both stay with him and you'll be safe.'

Tom looked relieved. 'I like Running Bear. He tells good stories.'

Jeff laughed and chucked him lightly under the chin.

'That's my boy! You keep your heart up and look after Maisie and I'll have Sarah back in no time at all!'

But his heart was heavy as he rode with the two children riding on his pack animal. Would Sarah be safe? And more importantly, could he get her back?

Running Bear hobbled to meet them as they rode into the medicine man's clearing. His wound was healing much quicker than any patient Jeff had treated during the war. It was amazing. But remembering the filthy conditions he'd worked under, perhaps it wasn't amazing after all.

He explained about Sarah, and Running Bear was glad to have the children's company. Jeff looked at the old man's wound and was pleased to see that the telltale red around the puckered edges was now gone. He smelled a pungent odour which reminded him of garlic and pine mixed with something he couldn't identify. He must remember to ask the old man what he used to promote such quick healing, when next he had time to smoke a pipe and hold one of those deep conversations they both enjoyed.

But now he must be away.

Then from a distance came a sighing wail which grew louder as they listened. Running Bear's hand on Jeff's arm prevented him from plunging into the undergrowth.

'Wait, my son. It is the cry of death. Do not intrude on private grief.'

'But . . .'

Running Bear shook his head. 'Have patience, White Hunter. Be as the Pawnees, for the one who grieves comes to us.'

'How do you know this, Running Bear?'

The old man smiled, a saddened experienced smile.

'I have lived long and I have taken to myself many persons' grief. I have absorbed it, dispersed it and given healing, not of the physical body but of the spirit. Healing isn't only a bodily thing, but must also be part of the etheric body. You understand me?'

'No, unfortunately I do not. I was trained to treat a body. I can take out a bullet, dress a wound, cut off a limb, deliver a child and give certain pills and potions, but I was never trained to treat a spirit!'

'Then you have much still to learn, my son. Someday, if the spirits are willing, you may know some part of what I can teach you. But now we wait.' He looked uneasy, his old weather-worn face screwed itself into a frown. Jeff had the curious feeling that he was seeing and hearing something that eluded Jeff's civilized ears.

Then Running Bear was waving him forward.

'You can go and meet the one in distress. She needs your help badly.'

'But how do you know it's a woman?'

'I know. Just go quickly.'

The narrow trail wound through the trees. It was the trail beaten out by those coming from the village to the old man's tipi for healing.

Jeff ran lightly and fast. He was impatient to find whoever needed help so that he was free to go look for Sarah.

So he was shocked to see Sun-in-the-Morning staggering towards him, with her new baby on her back, a small child by the hand, and a leather bag slung from one shoulder.

There was blood and smoke smeared on her cheek, and the small girl dripped blood from her head.

Jeff gasped, and sprang to the squaw's assistance.

'What is it? What's happened?' he asked as he took her weight and scooped up the child as he did so.

'They've burned down the village and killed everyone,' the woman said amidst tearing sobs. 'I was away from the village gathering wood and I watched and saw what happened. Moonflower was fetching water from the stream. We hid together, but when the men had gone, there was no one left but us!'

'Who were they? The white men from the camp?'

Sun-in-the-Morning nodded.

He examined the wound on the child's head.

'And this, and your wound, how did this happen?'

'We were hiding close by, and there

were some who tried to run away. Some of the white men were riding round and laughing and firing at them as if they were killing vermin! They fired into the bushes to see if anyone was hiding. I pulled Moonflower to the ground and held her down so that she couldn't run, but the bullets came like angry bees . . . '

Running Bear took Moonflower and proceeded to clean her wound, while Jeff lifted the sleeping baby in its reindeer hide cradle from Sun-in-the-Morning's back and laid it down safely; then he attended to the angry welt across her temple where the bullet had grazed. She would have a scar but she was alive. Never again would she be so near death and live.

He was conscious of Running Bear's continuous chanting as he worked on the child. It wasn't the usual thanking of the spirits of the forest, but more like an invocation designed to stir up both man and spirits to war.

When they had done all that was

possible for the patients, Jeff challenged Running Bear.

'What have you in mind, old friend?'

Running Bear looked at him grimly.

'What d'you think? I am old and unable to go to war, but I can invoke the help of our tribal spirits. The drums will beat tonight, and you must go and find Pana Hokan and you will tell him to fly like the wind and take possession of the Devil's Gorge for that is where the white men will make for. There, at the plateau it will all be settled. I can see it now ...'

Jeff looked at him curiously. The old man's black eyes had taken on a far-seeing opaque look. Jeff's spine tingled. He'd heard tales from lonely woodsmen about the strange abilities that some medicine men cultivated. Now he was seeing and hearing for himself.

'Can you see Sarah?' he asked, in a low quiet voice.

'Yes. I see her.'

Jeff's breath rasped in his throat. He hardly dared think never mind ask his next question.

'Is she safe and well?'

'She is frightened and angry. But at this time she is unmolested. There is an aura around her but a darkness presses in on her. But go, and take this with you.' He picked up a crude leather bag and handed it to Jeff.

'What is it?'

'Gunpowder. You will know what to do with it when the time comes.'

'How did you get it?' He opened the bag to look at the contents and recognized army issue.

The old man grinned.

'Taken from an army patrol during the war. Now it might be useful. Now, no more talk. Ride that way,' and he pointed east. 'That is where you will find the hunters. Tell Pana Hokan to ride like the wind, and *then* you can go seek your woman.'

It was easy following the trail of the hunters and soon, Jeff came upon them coming back to their village laden with game.

Pana Hokan lifted his hand to halt the procession, when he saw Jeff riding towards them.

'Ho there! What brings you in such a hurry your mare is lathered?'

'Pana Hokan, I am the bearer of bad news.' He outlined what had happened, and Pana Hokan raised his fists into the air in a token of grief and fury.

'What about Sun-in-the-Morning and our baby? I should go to them.'

'They are fine and Running Bear is looking after them.' Pana Hokan nodded and then turned and spoke rapidly to the Indians behind him. Their voices rose with anger and soon they were organized into two groups, the experienced braves to go on to the Devil's Gorge and the youngsters to take the kill back to their village and to look for those who might be lying wounded.

Jeff watched them go and then wheeled his horse and made for higher ground. Somewhere out there was Jasper Wirrel and Sarah. By now, he calculated, Wirrel would have caught up with his men. He tried putting himself in Wirrel's place. What would he do if he was Wirrel? He knew the answer. He would seek out the only man who had influence on the Pawnees and trade Sarah for sweeping the country of the unwanted red men.

But Jeff knew that Wirrel had made a mistake in firing the village and massacring the women and children as a warning to the other villages of what they might expect. It would take more than Jeff White Hunter to persuade the Pawnees to leave their tribal lands after such an outrage. His guess would be that even now the smoke would be rising and the fate of the village known.

Jasper Wirrel had been a reckless fool, but a reckless fool was a dangerous fool. If he couldn't get his own way, then he couldn't leave Sarah alive to testify to the kidnapping.

He had to find her before the

confrontation in the Devil's Gorge. That way, he could save the life of the slow-moving wagon train. If he didn't succeed, then Wirrel could obliterate all evidence and give those in Washington who were in the plot to take the land, the news they wanted. Lassiter too would be killed. He could see it all clearly.

Away ahead he saw the dust cloud formed by Pana Hokan's bunch of riders. They rode like the wind. Then he saw another hazy cloud far to the south. It could be Elijah Smith's posse on the track of the wagon train, and decided to ride parallel and fan out and look for Wirrel's sign.

The sun rose higher and Jeff sweated and, when he came to a narrow stream, he stopped and allowed the mare to drink and doused his head with a hatful of water before drinking himself. He checked his mount's feet, no problem there. To be on the safe side he walked her in the shallows before mounting up and moving on.

He was approaching the gorge and the sun was sinking fast, casting huge shadows, when Jeff got his first eerie feeling of premonition. It was all too quiet. No birds chirped or wheeled around for their last forage of the day. It was as if everything held its breath. He slowed to a cautious walk, his head swivelling from side to side as he came nearer to the rising jagged rocks that littered the ground before the entrance to the gorge.

He stopped amidst a mighty upheaval of stones that looked as if they'd been thrown down by a giant hand. He dismounted, and tied up the mare before climbing high and studying the darkening terrain through his glasses.

Nothing stirred in the canyon and yet he was uneasy. Suddenly there was a rattle of stones and the creaking of leather and Jeff looked behind him, and saw the snaking trail of a number of Indians but it wasn't Pana Hokan leading them but Jasper Wirrel, and close beside his horse, was Sarah on a packhorse bound and gagged, her blouse torn and her hair hanging in rat's-tails down her back.

Jeff's first impulse was to ride out and meet them, and shoot the bastard. Anger made him shake. At least she was still alive.

He considered shooting him from the rocks but the distance was too far and Sarah might get in the way. He saw the leading rein wrapped securely around Wirrel's pommel. If he was lucky enough to shoot Wirrel, she couldn't ride away and those desperate men behind Wirrel might just shoot her in revenge.

He watched helplessly as the small cavalcade entered the gorge. He followed on foot. There might be a chance when they neared the plateau, to cause a diversion and escape with Sarah into one of the many cracks and crannies that littered the sides of the ravine.

The little cavalcade was well into the gorge when the first shots came from both sides and at all angles. He caught a movement high up on the crag and saw one of Pana Hokan's Indians taking aim. By God, he'd made it! Jeff's heart lifted and then dropped again as Wirrel, firing wildly, rowelled his horse and made off up the canyon towards the plateau with Sarah's horse galloping behind.

'Oh, God! No!' There was no way he could follow as shots were exchanged and horses cannoned into each other as the panicky riders aimed for targets they couldn't see.

Jeff scrambled up to a vantage point and took out a couple of men and then ducked as a fusillade of shots came his way. Then Pana Hokan was scrambling from behind a rearing needle of rock waving his arm as a signal and then before Jeff's astonished eyes, a ragged line of Indians came leaping over the crest of the hill, hollering and screaming at the men below.

He took one look, saw the devastation going on and scrambled down to find his horse. He must get after Wirrel and

Sarah. The man must not escape!

The trail snaked through the pass, gradually climbing a gradient punishing to his mount. If it was affecting his mare, then the other horses must be suffering too. His glimpse of Sarah on the packhorse meant that her horse was carrying much more weight and would hold Wirrel back. That thought made his heart race. If Wirrel thought the situation dangerous enough, he might kill Sarah outright and disappear into one of the many canyons leading from the mountain range.

Jeff clenched his teeth. He'd find Sarah if it took forever and if she was dead, he'd never rest until he had the bastard staked out and at the mercy of his surgeon's hands. It would be fitting to use him for experiments usually performed on cadavers . . .

He watched the trail carefully, noting disturbed stones on hard ground. Once he was lucky and found horseshoe prints galloping over marshy ground, one set of prints heavier than the other.

They were moving fast, and Jeff raised his head, sniffing the wind. Was there smoke somewhere ahead?

He moved cautiously, giving the mare a breather as his eyes followed the faint track which had now left the main trail. Perhaps Wirrel expected to hide Sarah away in some cave and go back to his men and negotiate for Jeff's help to calm down the Pawnees and persuade them to leave their lands.

Some hope in that, he thought grimly. Burning one of their villages and killing their women and children wasn't the way to get rid of them. Wirrel certainly didn't understand the Indian mentality. They would endure any hardship, take defeat stoically, understanding that it was all the will of the Great Spirit to test their courage in adversity, but to humiliate them, harm their women and children was another matter entirely. It reflected on their honour and their prowess in battle.

The Pawnees were not to be browbeaten.

His senses were fine-tuned as, slowly, he and the mare moved forward. He saw the mare's ears prick and quietly dismounted, throwing the reins over a bush. Then he hunched low and easing the trigger guard on his rifle, he inched forward. A flock of birds rose flapping their wings above the trees which startled him. His rifle came up but again all was still.

He came to a narrow fast-flowing stream and decided to follow it upwards. If Wirrel was aiming to burrow out a place to stash Sarah, then it would be beside water.

He climbed steadily and the air became thinner and he was gasping, his lungs working hard when he came upon the sudden dip in the ground and he was looking down at a huge basin surrounded by hills and far down below was a sprawling ranchhouse and lean-to buildings and a herd of horses grazing on fresh green grass, no doubt kept green from hidden springs from which poured the narrow stream.

'Well, I'll be damned!' Jeff muttered, and that was all he remembered for a crashing pain on the back of his head splintered into blackness and a host of stars which swirled into a void.

He groaned and his head was fit to burst. What the hell? He must have had too much of Running Bear's potent liquor. He passed a hand over his head and his fingers probed where the pain hurt most. He encountered a sticky swelling, his hair stiff and encrusted with dried blood.

Cold-cocked! Then he remembered. It all came back. The trekking and the climbing and then the amazing sight of a small valley tucked away in the hills and the ranch which looked as if it had been there for some time and the herd of horses grazing quietly. It must be Jasper Wirrel's place, a lonely, secret hideout, an insurance against the Washington plans going wrong. Or had Jasper Wirrel led a double life and those smartasses in Washington never knew they were dealing with a man who dealt outside the law?

He had no time to figure it out, for he was being hauled roughly to his feet and dragged from the foul-smelling outhouse across a yard and thrown down before the veranda of the rough pine-timber shack.

He looked up at the man who stood wide-legged over him, and twisted as Wirrel's foot took him in the ribs. The blow would have shattered bone if he hadn't moved instinctively.

'So you're back with us, Doctor Potter. I was afraid Benny here had shattered your skull, but you kept snuffling which made me think your skull was harder than I thought.' He looked at Benny and smiled thinly. 'Which is a good thing for Benny. I don't like mistakes, and I need you, Doctor Potter.'

'Go to hell!'

Wirrel frowned. 'In my own good time, Doctor.'

'If you think I've any influence on the Pawnees after what your men did

162

in that village, you're sadly wrong! You and your men will never leave their territory alive! It's a wonder they haven't come here!'

Wirrel shrugged. 'Not here. The Pawnees consider this valley haunted. They call it Death Valley.'

'So? How long can you stay here, holed up against the tribes you've united with the burning of the village and the massacre of the women and children?'

'I've got your wife here, Doctor Potter. I'm not a fool, you know. I realize my men went too far. Now I want you to negotiate with Pana Hokan to let us out of here. He can have the herd and whatever is on the ranch. He must have some feeling for your wife. He'll not want to see her killed. I want a safe passage.'

'You mean you're giving up your plan to rid the land of the Pawnees?'

Wirrel's eyes flickered and Jeff's spine tingled. There was something wrong, but his head pounded too hard to figure

163

out what it might be.

'Yes. You and your wife's life for a free passage for me and my men. We'll head on back to Washington.'

'How do I know she's unharmed?'

'You can see her for yourself.'

Jeff dragged himself upright, head swimming, stomach heaving and when Wirrel turned and went into the ranchhouse, Jeff followed into the dim interior.

There, blinking and adjusting his sight, he saw Sarah bound to a rough wooden chair. Her head was bent and her shoulders slumped and her bodice and skirt were torn and her hair hung about her shoulders. Jeff staggered forward and lifted her chin, staring into her white, drawn face. Her eyes were closed.

'Sarah, sweetheart, it's Jeff.' Slowly her eyes opened. Jeff saw the sudden fear turn to joy.

'Oh, Jeff!' Then the tears came and he held her close for a moment and then reached for his knife to cut her free, but a strong grip on his wrist stayed him.

'Not so fast, Doctor. You've got to do your bit first. You've got to talk to Pana Hokan first.'

'I'll talk to him, but I'll take her with me,' Jeff said firmly. 'You can send as many men as you like with me, but she goes too.'

Wirrel stroked his chin and Benny whispered in his ear and Wirrel laughed.

'Right. We'll do as you say, Benny. You're in charge.'

Jeff looked from one to another.

'What goes on? You know what will happen if Sarah or I are killed? There'll be no stopping the Pawnees. There'll be an all-out war and it won't be only you and your men, it'll be all those wagon trains coming through, like the one which is coming through the Devil's Gorge sometime soon.'

Jasper Wirrel smiled.

'That one, is one that will disappear from the face of the earth and the

Pawnees will get the blame.'

'You think so? How many men do you think you've got left out there? How many men do you reckon are lying unburied in the Devil's Gorge?'

Wirrel licked his lips. 'Blue Jay took only part of the crew. There's Lassiter and the rest of the men.'

Jeff laughed grimly. 'You made a mistake when you beat up Lassiter. He's not a man who'll take that treatment lying down. You're living in a fool's world, Wirrel.'

Wirrel sprang at Jeff, but now Jeff was recovering fast. His head pounded, but his reflexes were back to normal. He dodged the fist aimed at his jaw and rocked Wirrel back on his heels with a sharp clip on the cheekbone.

'Why you . . . !' thundered Wirrel which brought the men running to watch with interest at a fight in the offing.

Jeff crouched low, hands wide apart, fingers gesturing.

'Come on, you bastard, come and

166

get me. Let's see what kind of man you are without your guns and your men to do your dirty work!'

There was a murmur from the crowd, speculation mounting as Wirrel hesitated. Then Wirrel sprang to the back of Sarah's chair. He laughed savagely as he drew his gun and thrust it hard against her neck.

'Back off, Doctor Potter, or even you won't be able to put her together again!'

There was an audible gasp from amongst the men and slowly they moved away with only Benny remaining. Jeff breathed deeply and looked into Sarah's eyes. He saw her love and trust in him and it drew from him a renewed strength. He couldn't allow her to lose that trust.

For a long moment there was silence. It was as if they were all frozen and then Jeff spoke.

'I'll talk to Pana Hokan, but Sarah goes with me or the deal's off.' He nodded to Benny. 'We'll be safe enough. Benny here can bring a couple of heavies and I know their guns will be trained on us at all times. I'm not going to do anything foolish. That's the deal. Take it or leave it!'

9

Elijah Smith drew up his horse and raised his glasses and studied the moving wagon train ahead. A telltale cloud of dust followed behind. He could see small figures walking alongside the wagons. All seemed quiet. Elijah gave a sigh of relief. Wirrel, the bastard, hadn't caught up with the train. He wondered why. They were now approaching the Devil's Gorge.

Perhaps Blue Jay had held back, waiting for the boss. He raked the surrounding terrain for any hint of movement. Wirrel must be out there with the woman.

Tod Lewis eased his mount towards him and screwing his eyes up against the glare, located the moving wagon train.

'That the one we're lookin' for, Elijah?'

'Yeah. How many goddamn trains are there in these parts?' He spoke sharply. It had gone through his mind that if Blue Jay was holed up waiting to attack, then he had a problem. He had to choose between helping to defend the train against his own buddies, or stand aside and watch a massacre.

He cursed. He'd figured on catching up with the train much earlier, and advising the train boss to cut across country and travel through the mountain range from the next valley. A longer circuit but safe. There was no need to divulge Wirrel's plans. They need never know that they had been saved from certain death.

Now, they were plodding along, within a halfday's march of the gorge and into a trap. Elijah imagined the men waiting, grumbling, and cleaning rifles and living on hard tack because they couldn't light fires.

He felt sick to his stomach.

Tod Lewis spat.

'What we do, Elijah? You're bossin'

this little mutiny. Wirrel ain't goin' to be pleased we lighted out to warn that bunch.'

Elijah looked at him grimly, his mind made up for him.

'What else can we do? I told you all what Lassiter told me. We all want land, but not to murder for it! Wirrel won't allow anyone to live who can go back to Washington and testify against him.'

Tod Lewis moved uneasily. 'Are you saying . . . ?'

'Yeah, that's what I'm saying. Any of us who don't go along with him a hundred per cent will have to watch his back. We've already made our stand.'

'I'd better talk to the boys.' Tod turned his horse and he and the other cowboys went into a huddle. Then he returned to Elijah who was moodily watching the wagon train.

'They're goin' along with you, Elijah. They don't mind persuadin' the reds to leave their huntin' grounds but not to kill white folk. So do we catch up with 'em and escort 'em through the pass?'

Elijah sighed. He wasn't a fighting man. On the other hand he wasn't the kind to shirk a scrap, if he had a chance, that is.

'Right! We'd better get movin' and catch up and have a pow-wow with that wagon boss and put him in the picture.'

Three hours later, Bert Kiernan pulled up the wagon train and waited for the bunch of men travelling at a fast lope.

'Something amiss, fellers?' Bert looked from one to another, his rifle at the ready.

Elijah slid from his horse and advanced, hand outstretched.

'I'm Elijah Smith; we met at Wirrel's camp.'

'Ah, the land commission men. I remember now. I saw you at the camp-fire.' Bert Kiernan relaxed. He waved at the other men and they came crowding around while the women and children peeped out of wagons or watched from

172

wagon seats. They all looked tired and dusty. Bert turned to them. 'You folk can take time out to make camp. I think we've gone far enough today.' Then, to the men, 'We'll tackle the gorge at dawn, and take all day, after the horses have been rested.'

'That's what we're here about. We'll escort you through the pass.'

Bert Kiernan stared at him. 'What the hell for? We're quite capable of tackling the pass. It's not the first one, you know.'

'Look, I'm not goin' into details, but there's danger.'

'What? From the Pawnees? I was made to understand that the Indians hereabouts were friendly. How come there's danger?'

'Not from Indians.'

'You don't say there's outlaws in these parts? Why, man, we're not worth robbing. We've tools and grub and a few sticks of furniture and very little else. I don't figure we have more than a few hundred dollars between us. We got our land grants . . . ' He looked sharply at Elijah. 'That boss of yours isn't after our bits of paper, is he?'

'Nope!'

'Then where's the danger coming from?'

Elijah hesitated. Then he spoke slowly and distinctly.

'We don't go along with what Wirrel planned. He's going to get these Kansas lands in any way he can.'

'How are we involved? It's none of our business.'

'He thinks it is. You've got grants and you could be witnesses . . . '

'Of what, for God's sake?'

'Of murder, of land grabbing and whatever else he's mixed up in. We're only a few of his men. The rest are hidden up there in the pass and they're waiting for you, and you'll not get through. The evidence will be left and the Pawnees blamed for reprisals because of the burning of the village and the massacre.'

'Massacre?' Kiernan looked horrified

and there was a protesting growl from the men listening.

'Yep. Wirrel ordered the attack. You happened along at the wrong time. In Wirrel's eyes you're nothing, just another wagon train held up by Indians.'

'Can't we bypass the gorge?'

'Nope! This is the only trail through these hills. You could have turned off two days ago. I figured we might have caught up with you earlier.'

'We were travelling at night, making forced marches. We wanted to get the pass behind us.' Kiernan looked ahead into the distance where the rocks reared up and the Gorge began. 'You say they're already there? How many men?'

'Eighteen or twenty.'

Kiernan rasped his chin. 'And we've got seven men and two boys and you're' — he counted Elijah's men — 'ten of you. We might just make it, now we're warned. I was in the army. We could make a plan. The

women and kids will have to lie in
the bottom of the wagons surrounded
by sacks of dry goods and we'll have
to redistribute the barrels to protect the
drivers.'

Molly Kiernan, who'd been listening,
drew near.

'The kids can lie down. Us women
will drive. We're all drivers. We'll do
our bit.'

'You could catch a slug.'

'We'll take our chances. You can't
drive and shoot. You'd be sitting
targets. This way we'd have a chance.'

Kiernan grunted. His wife was right
as usual.

'Right. We'll eat and then we get
down to organizing ourselves.' He stuck
out his hand to Elijah. 'I'm mighty
grateful, mister. You could have turned
a blind eye.'

The sun's first rays were hardly
turning the hilltops pink when the
wagon train moved off with Elijah
and his men riding herd on them.
They moved slowly ahead, now wary

and watchful. A crying child was soon quietened and there was nothing but the creak of leather and squeaky wheels travelling over hard ground.

Then came the sound that froze them in their tracks. The sound of a deep bass drum. Elijah spurred his horse ahead to where Bert Kiernan led the little cavalcade.

'What d'you make of that?'

Kiernan shook his head and looked around. All was still in the grey light of dawn.

'Someone's awake and it ain't no white man.'

They listened as the drum beat grew louder and sharper, with pauses and trills and another drum, with a vibrant quality about it, answered.

'Hell! They're talkin' to each other!' Elijah said hoarsely.

Kiernan shook his head. 'I've heard drums like that before. It's a call to council. There's something up.'

'It's coming from inside the gorge. Hell! Wirrel should be in there with the rest of the men! What's happened to them?'

Kiernan shrugged.

'Your guess is as good as mine. But it doesn't sound good for them. What we do? Go on or stop here?'

'I suppose we go on. It's not a rallying sound. It don't sound like they're workin' themselves up into a frenzy.'

'Holy Mother of God! Look at that!' As the sun burst over the hills in streaks of morning glory, they saw the line of Indians appear like magic. They stood straight and tall and as they watched, a bunch of riders appeared in the mouth of the gorge. All were resplendent in eagles' feathers and they carried rifles. Their leader rode ahead, warbonnet fanning out, making him into an impressive figure. He controlled his horse with his knees only for in one hand he carried his rifle and in the other he carried an eight-foot lance decorated with coloured feathers.

Elijah and Keirnan watched them

come and when they were near enough, Elijah rode forward, one hand held high in friendly greeting.

Pana Hokan waved to his braves to stay, and he moved on to meet Elijah. He lifted his own hand in greeting.

'I come in peace and with a warning. I am Pana Hokan of the Pawnees. Who are you?'

'I am Elijah Smith, once a member of Jasper Wirrel's expedition, but not any more.'

'You took part in the massacre?' For a moment Pana Hokan looked grim.

'No sir! Me and these men came to escort this wagon train through the pass. We had fears that this wagon train was going to be ambushed.'

Pana Hokan nodded slowly. 'So that was why they came into the pass so carelessly without sending scouts, a sign of bad leadership.' Pana Hokan smiled briefly. 'They rode into an ambush. We were waiting, but their leader got away with a woman prisoner. His name is Wirrel. You know him?'

Elijah nodded. 'He was the boss, but me and these fellers didn't like what he was aimin' to do. Where's he headin' for now?'

'We've got him holed up in a camp beyond the gorge. It is what you call a stand-off. We are waiting to parlay with him. The white medicine man must get his woman back.'

'Then we should ride with you. He's a bastard and will kill a woman as readily as he would a redskin . . . beggin' your pardon, chief.'

Pana Hokan bowed with dignity, a rueful expression flickering across his face.

'Granted. I am well aware that white men regard us as less than human, rather as animals. Words mean nothing.' He made a short sharp gesture as if to cut the words short.

'I'm sorry, chief. Where did you learn your English so good?'

They were riding along together now, the two little bands amalgamated, albeit with suspicion on both sides.

'I lived with a white family for two years and went to school with white children.'

'Why did you do that?'

'Because a white man saved my father's life and as he was a wise man, he thought it would be a good thing to find out about these strange newcomers who could show mercy as well as cruelty. It made it easier to understand them when I returned and told him of my experiences.'

'Huh! So your father was one of those who went to Washington to speak of peace proposals?'

'And failed. He found the men of Washington talk with forked tongues and make promises they do not keep!'

For a moment Pana Hokan's eyes flashed and his nostrils curled and Elijah wished he'd kept his mouth shut.

Then Pana Hokan smiled.

'But there are good white men. We are going to help one of them now. Doctor White Hunter is a good man and he has helped my people and when we rid this land of these bad white men, we can return to a peaceful way of living.' Then he frowned. 'But we can never be the same again. The loss of our women and children and the undignified way our old ones died . . . Ee . . . aaa! We must not dwell on what is done but think of the future!'

They travelled slowly up the trail, passing horses and men lying in postures of death. Elijah's lips tightened. It had been some fight. Here and there were the bodies of Indians. Already they were being gathered up and taken away for burial.

They made faster time once through the pass, and soon they came to the head of another valley where down below they could see the hidden ranchhouse.

All around waited Pana Hokan's braves who were all watching the white doctor and his woman being escorted at gun point up the narrow incline towards them.

One of the men shouted in a stentorian voice, 'Ho there, Chief Pana Hokan! Doctor Potter wants to parlay with you.' They stopped within shouting distance and the man waved to warn them all to remain at a safe distance. 'Any sudden movements and the woman gets it!' The gun that had been at Sarah's back suddenly appeared at her neck.

'What is it you want?' called Pana Hokan.

Jeff looked from Sarah to Benny, who was pinning her close to him and digging the barrel of his gun into her neck making her gasp with pain.

'Back off, Benny! Sarah's going nowhere, so let her loose!' He glared at Benny whose lips curled back from his teeth in his enjoyment of the situation. Benny drew pleasure from a woman's pain. Then his lips came together in a snarl and he crushed her to him before hurling her to the ground. Then, standing wide-legged he pointed his gun at her as she lay gasping and holding her ribs.

'One wrong move, Doctor, from you or anyone here and she's dead! Do you hear?' He looked around wildly at the watching braves and Pana Hokan and lastly at Elijah Smith. Slowly and deliberately he spat in Elijah's direction. 'As for you, Elijah Smith, the boss has special plans for you! He don't like turncoats!'

Elijah laughed.

'Hark at the cockerel! Wirrel's got you believin' he's God and you're his archangel! You don't rate in my eyes, Benny Fry. You're just a dogsbody doin' Wirrel's dirty work. If you were half a man you'd let the doctor and the woman go!'

'I've got my orders and I aim to carry them out. There's too much at stake to cross Wirrel. You should know that. Now say your piece, Doctor, and make it good.'

Pana Hokan stepped forward and Benny's gun came up.

'That's far enough, Chief.' He nodded to Jeff Potter.

Jeff licked his lips. He still hadn't figured what he might do to outfox Benny without risking Sarah's life. One thing for sure he wasn't going back down there quietly if Pana Hokan turned down his proposals.

'Jasper Wirrel wants this land. He wants all the Pawnee hunting territory and he wants you, Pana Hokan, to show an example to the other lodges and go quietly.'

Pana Hokan's back stiffened as he heard these words.

'And if I do not choose to do so?'

'Then it will be war with the soldiers from Washington. Already a large military unit is coming to the aid of Wirrel and his men. It is part of the plan to occupy this state, build a new fort and create new towns and farmsteads.'

'It is our land! It has been ever since the Great Spirit looked down and saw it was good land and gave it to us!

Would the white men go against the Great Spirit?'

'I'm sorry. I am but the bearer of Wirrel's plans. Wirrel is authorized by those in power in Washington. But those men are corrupt. Wirrel himself runs with certain outlaws . . . '

'He runs with the buffalo as well as the hunters?'

'Yeah, you might say that. You have a choice, Pana Hokan. Leave this country and find another, or risk more deaths amongst your people.'

'I have no choice, Doctor White Hunter, just as you have no choice. We both have chosen our paths in life and we must follow them.' He turned to Benny Fry. 'The answer is no! Tell your chief that it is war to the death!'

Just then the deep bass drum began to boom and the rhythmic vibrations hurt the ears. Benny started, his gunhand outstretched as he whirled around, wild-eyed, let rip a couple of shots that went wild. It was then Elijah Smith coolly raised his rifle and shot him like shooting a fox in a barnyard.

Then all was pandemonium. Jeff dived on Sarah and rolled over her, protecting her body as the two accompanying bodyguards fumbled for their weapons. A fusillade of slugs hummed like angry bees and slammed into them, punching them backwards like unseen fists.

Then Jeff was cradling Sarah in his arms and she was trembling and clinging to him as if she would never let him go again.

A great cheer went up and Pana Hokan, a smile on his usually grave face was standing over them.

'Your woman is unharmed, White Hunter?'

Jeff nodded. At that moment he couldn't speak. Relief that she was now safe, overwhelmed him.

'Then we go and dig out this man Wirrel from his lair.' Pana Hokan's tone was grim. 'He and his men must pay for the deaths of my people.'

'I shall come with you, Pana Hokan. There will be work for me.'

Pana Hokan nodded gravely. 'See to your woman and follow, if that is your wish.'

Jeff held out a hand to him.

'Thank you. You have been a true friend.'

'You forget, you are one of us now and always will be. We need men like you if we are to prosper in this new world the white men are creating.' There was infinite sadness in his words. Jeff realized that for Pana Hokan, the careless, free days of his youth would never return.

Then Pana Hokan was galloping away and, with a shout and a wave of his arm, the Pawnee braves followed him down into the valley below. They fanned out and as Jeff Potter watched alongside Elijah Smith and his men, they saw them encircle the ranchhouse and their warcries came back faintly on the breeze.

Elijah Smith watched, his lips pursed, a frown on his face and he shook his head and turned away.

'I can't watch. Some of those men down there were buddies. They weren't all bad. They were just swayed by greed as I was in the beginning. It seemed the chance of a lifetime to get a stake together and make a good life for ourselves.'

'But you saw the light! Those fellers down there were prepared to do murder!'

Elijah sighed. 'Yeah, well they're goin' to pay now, aren't they?'

Jeff watched the Indians streaming down from the hills until the valley floor was choked with riders all screaming like devils and when the firing started and the first smoke and flames flared up, he held Sarah close to him so that she should not see the carnage.

Much later when it was all over he left Sarah with Elijah.

'Look after her for me. There's work for me down there.'

He found many injured among the dying. Already the dead were being carried away. There was only one surviving white man and he was tied on a long rope behind Pana Hokan's horse. It was a smoke-blackened Jasper Wirrel, with puffy eyes and a cut forehead and one leg stuck out at an unusual angle. One side of him was already skinned by Pana Hokan dragging him behind him, as the chief gave orders.

The sun was setting across the valley when finally Jeff straightened his aching back and found Pana Hokan still astride his horse, watching him.

'You have done well, White Hunter. I am pleased with you.'

Jeff wiped the sweat from his forehead.

'I can't say the same for you, chief.'

Pana Hokan raised his eyebrows.

'Oh? And why do you say that?'

'Was there any need to drag Wirrel after you like a dog?'

'He *is* a dog. He merits nothing less.'

'Maybe. But do you have to play the savage? Torturing your enemies will never bring about a real peace between the white men and yourselves!'

Pana Hokan bent down and stared into Jeff's eyes.

'What would you have done if your woman had been killed by this man? Tell me that, eh?'

Jeff's eyes fell and he shrugged his shoulders defeatedly.

'I suppose something very similar.' He sighed. 'What do you do to him now?'

'Take him to the justice seat on the plateau. There he will be tried and all the sub chiefs will be there.'

'And he'll be sentenced to death?'

'Of course. But justice must be seen by all.'

'Very well. But do me a favour, chief. Put him on a horse. Don't drag him there, or there won't be a body left, never mind a dead man!'

Pana Hokan gave him a long, assessing look.

'You're a good man, White Hunter. I'll do as you say.' He gestured to one of his braves who caught a riderless horse and the unconscious Jasper Wirrel was strapped on its back.

Then as the ranchhouse and buildings burned, the excited victorious Indians turned back towards the Devil's Gorge and the plateau where justice had been carried out for hundreds of years.

10

The long straggling line of riders slowly snaked their way through the pass into the Devil's Gorge. High up on the mighty cliffs that reared on each side of the gorge itself stood riders at attention, proud and straightbacked and all with eight-foot lances in one hand and rifles in the other.

They were immobile, paying homage to Pana Hokan and waiting to see justice done to the man who had ordered the massacre of the Pawnee village.

Lazy smoke from many hilltop fires had blazoned the message bringing tribal members from far and wide. And in the background beat the deep bass tribal drum calling all to the justice ground.

Running Bear was waiting for the prisoner. He'd been brought by his grandson and other youths of the tribe in a travois. Now he waited, his old weathered face inscrutable. He knew what had to be done.

Then at last the cavalcade halted. The long slow gradient had brought them out on to the plateau from which the whole length and breadth of the gorge could be seen. It had been used as a lookout place in the old days when tribe warred against tribe. Now it was just a bleak windswept rock, haunted and dismal as if the spirits still grieved and howled when the wind was high.

Jasper Wirrel raised his head. It was an effort. His clothes were torn and where he had been dragged over the rough ground, his flesh resembled raw meat. He licked dry lips, his eyes unnaturally bright.

'Where am I?' he croaked, and his head wagged from side to side. Then his eyes lit on Jeff Potter. 'Doctor, for the love of God, help me!'

'Your God won't help you now!' Pana Hokan's voice boomed and echoed in the gorge. 'You are here to pay the penalty for your crimes. You ordered your men to burn our village when our men were away hunting. You ordered the deaths of our women and children and our old people.'

'That's a lie! It was Lassiter's idea! He's the one you want!' There was a murmur of angry voices and a young man leapt forward with a knife in his hand. Wirrel's horse kicked out, jarring Wirrel who groaned and he was helpess against the attack. The knife sliced down his face and blood gushed before his assailant was dragged away.

The horse was haltered and Wirrel's bonds cut free and he was dragged towards a thin pinnacle of rock and bound so that he could see the long narrow slash in the earth which was the gorge.

He looked about him. Far above him the lazy black vultures wheeled with instinctive patience. His mouth was dry, his head pounded and his guts turned to water.

'I tell you, you've got the wrong man!' But his words were whipped away on the wind.

Running Bear hobbled forward and stood before him.

'You're a liar and a coward, Jasper Wirrel. Have you forgotten me? I was the first man you shot, remember? You shot an old man without warning and you laughed.'

'If you kill me, the army will kill you all! Even now they are on the way here. Any rebellion will be put down with the strongest force! It could be genocide for all you people!'

Now he was breathing deeply as the men surrounding him began to growl in their throats. Suddenly a lance was thrown, a perfect arc through the air, a silent menace. It scraped Wirrel's thigh and thunked into the ground behind. Wirrel struggled to free himself as the animal-like growl sharpened. To Jeff Potter, it sounded like a collective animal suddenly out of control and smelling blood.

Then, it started. The lances thrown but not to kill but to wound. Jeff fought his way to Pana Hokan.

'You said there would be no torture! What the hell is this?'

Pana Hokan shrugged.

'These men have all lost someone, wives and children and parents. I can't stop them!'

'Then loosen his bonds and let him run! That is what you do with evil-doers, isn't it? Give him a chance like you do your own prisoners.'

For a long moment Pana Hokan considered him and then looked at the bloodied man hanging there with the ever-growing pile of spears around him and the spurting wounds that were now like fully opened blossoms. He nodded his head.

'He's had enough. The rest is up to him.' He held up his hands and the lances ceased to fly. Then moving forward himself he cut Wirrel's bonds.

'Now run. But if I were you, I'd take the quick way out.' Pana Hokan gestured over the cliff edge. Wirrel looked at him, wide-eyed and frothing at the mouth.

'Damn you to hell!' he roared and, breathing deeply, he mustered his strength and sprang forward and took a great leap into space.

The men crowded forward and watched as the body kicked and twisted as it went down and down. Then a great howl went up and suddenly stopped and the drum with it. The sudden silence hurt the ears. Only the wind soughed and whined and in the sky was the sound of lazy flapping wings . . .

It was over. Jeff Potter had never felt so exhausted in his life, not even during the worst of the fighting during the war. His thoughts turned to Sarah. He must get back and they must rebuild their life together. He'd build a bigger cabin for now there were future children to think of. All he wanted was to hold her close and tell her he loved her.

Colonel Cartwright leading his detail along the main trail pulled up his men.

'What do you make of that, Captain?'

'Looks like there's been a fire in these parts. I'll send the sergeant and half a dozen men to reconnoitre.'

'Do that, Captain, and we'll take a break. This is ass-blistering work. Goddamn Wirrel and those Washington shysters for stirring up trouble! There's no Pawnees in these parts. We haven't seen a goddamn one!'

The colonel and the captain shared a bottle while they waited for news. It was a couple of hours before a panting sergeant returned.

'Well, Sergeant, what's happened out there?'

'A burnt-out village, sir. It looks as if Wirrel doesn't need our help. He's got those redskins on the run.'

The colonel laughed.

'Good for him. That accounts for no

Indians hassling us. So, Captain, we can turn round and go back to Washington and report all's well and you can take your lady to the governor's ball.'

'Yessir! I should think we're both due some leave, after this trek. What do you say, sir?'

The colonel's eyes twinkled.

'Now you do come up with some good ideas sometimes, Charles.'

'I like to be helpful.'

'Then pour me another drink and one for yourself.'

The colonel stretched, his camp chair creaked.

'You know, if it wasn't for the damned Indians, I'd quite like this camp-fire lark!'

The captain looked about him.

'Plenty of fresh air, sir, but you can't beat Washington. I'll take the fug of Washington any day, and the ladies of course, bless their hearts!'

'Ah well, we'll soon be back amongst them. Any liquor left in that bottle, Charles?'

'Yes, sir. Enough for a couple of snorts.'

The colonel sighed with satisfaction.

'Charles, I think the time might be ripe for your promotion. A word in the right place . . . '

'Yes, sir?'

'Now as I see it, with everything well in hand and the country quiet and Wirrel doing his job properly, the powers-that-be will look kindly on your application. Now, if we get down to doing those reports and you're good at the paperwork, God knows where it might lead to . . . '

'Yessir! Between us we can make a good report . . . ' The voices faded on the night air.

Far away, an owl hooted and there was movement in the woods.

Other titles in the
Linford Western Library

THE CROOKED SHERIFF
John Dyson

Black Pete Bowen quit Texas with
a burning hatred of men who try
to take the law into their own
hands. But he discovers that things
aren't much different in the silver
mountains of Arizona.

THEY'LL HANG BILLY
FOR SURE:
Larry & Stretch
Marshall Grover

Billy Reese, the West's most notorious
desperado, was to stand trial. From
all compass points came the curious
and the greedy, the riff-raff of the
frontier. Suddenly, a crazed killer
was on the loose — but the Texas
Trouble-Shooters were there, girding
their loins for action.